Praise for Kate Perry's Novels

"Perry's storytelling skills just keep getting better and better!"

–Romantic Times Book Reviews

"Can't wait for the next in this series...simply great reading. Another winner by this amazing author."

–Romance Reviews Magazine

"Exciting and simply terrific."

–Romancereviews.com

"Kate Perry is on my auto buy list."

–Night Owl Romance

"A winning and entertaining combination of humor and pathos."

–Booklist

Other Titles by Kate Perry

The Laurel Heights Series:

Perfect for You

Close to You

Return to You

Looking for You

Dream of You

Sweet on You

The Family and Love Series:

Project Date

Playing Doctor

Playing for Keeps

Project Daddy

The Guardians of Destiny Series:

Marked by Passion

Chosen by Desire

Tempted by Fate

Dream of You

Kate Perry

Phoenix Rising Enterprise, Inc.

A super HUGE thank you hug to Lord Martha. She runs my world with an iron fist, and I love it.

Big, sloppy kisses to Julie and Parisa. And also to Josie, who knows when I need my coffee spiked.

And, as always, for my Magic Man. Smooches, my love.

Chapter One

As SHE STARED at the ceiling of her agent's office, Lola cursed her mother for naming her Lola Carmichael.

What had she been thinking? Maybe all those birth hormones had made the woman shortsighted. She obviously hadn't realized that a name like Lola Carmichael would severely limit a girl's career choices. An accountant named Lola? No way. It didn't help that she looked like Fantasy Time Barbie. She'd been relegated to being either a stripper or romance novelist straight out of the womb.

Guess which she became.

Lola slouched in the seat until her butt perched on the edge and her head rested on top of the chair back. Sighing, she counted the cracks in the ceiling as she waited.

She got up to twenty-three before she lost count.

"With all the money you make off me, shouldn't you be able to afford to fix the ceiling, Paul?"

Her agent didn't bother acknowledging her, his full attention on her manuscript.

She studied him as he read. Paul Jennings was the most unlikely looking agent she'd ever seen. If she had to cast him in a book, he'd be an ex-Navy sergeant—a hulk who dressed in fine suits, French cuffed shirts, and silk ties.

His office looked like him, too. The lines were simple and the colors muted, but all together it looked sharp and expensive.

One manicured hand flipped a page. Lola wondered what he thought of her story.

She didn't have to wonder long. Paul set it down and stared at her with dark, piercing eyes.

Since he didn't seem inclined to speak, she ventured a comment. "It has promise, don't you think?"

"It's shit."

"Don't hold back. Tell me like it is."

Paul leaned back in his chair and crossed his arms over his barrel chest. "Lola, you have six weeks until the deadline, and you just handed me three of the worst chapters you've ever written. Your first novel

was better than this."

"They aren't *that* bad."

"Lola, it's shit," he repeated distinctly.

"It needs some editing but—"

He picked up a page and read out loud. "'*All men were bastards. At least hers would be good looking, even if his chin was weak.*'"

She shrugged. "The hero has to have some flaws."

"This hero is more than flawed." He picked up the pages and tossed them into the garbage. "This hero is an asshole."

"I made him realistic," she said as she reached into the garbage and retrieved the chapters, slipping them into her bag for later.

Paul heaved a sigh and ran a hand over his face. "Isn't it time you got over Kevin?"

Her spine stiffened automatically. "This has nothing to do with Kevin."

"It has everything to do with him. You're bashing your hero because one man hurt you."

"He did not hurt me."

Paul cocked a brow.

Humiliated, yes. Hurt, hell no. A woman had to care to be hurt, and there was no way Lola cared about Kevin. Looking back, she wasn't sure she ever did. "I'm not hurt."

Paul didn't look like he believed her but he didn't argue. Instead, he got all business-like. "Fact of the matter is you have a deadline in six weeks and you've delivered nothing your editor will accept. Unless you want to destroy your career after all the hard work to get to this point, I'd suggest you get cracking and churn out one of the romance novels you're famous for."

That was the problem. She wrote her stories based on real-life happily-ever-afters. Her first book had been a veiled account of her parents' courtship, and every story since had been inspired by true stories of love.

This next book was supposed to be *her* story.

Until Kevin dumped her.

Not exactly the greatest romance to write about.

But what was she supposed to do? Scrap the whole story and start over? She didn't have another romance to replace her story. And, frankly, it was crazy to start over with the deadline six weeks away. If she could just make it to the ending, then she could go back and fix it all.

In theory.

Knowing Paul was waiting for some reply, she nodded. "I've got it all under control."

He didn't look like he believed her. "Get the old Lola Carmichael back. That's what people pay for. That's what put your current release at number eight on *New York Times* bestseller list."

Right.

"Speaking of your current bestseller." Paul grabbed one of the neatly filed folders on the corner of his desk and opened it. "Your publicist has booked you to speak on *Ladies' Night* this Friday at 8pm. You're helping launch the new radio show. They were excited to have you."

"Super," she said unenthusiastically as she took the information from him. "What am I supposed to talk about?"

He gave her that flat, no-nonsense look. "About your books, Lola. About romance, love, and whatever else the callers ask you about."

She made a face. "I'm not qualified."

"You're a bestselling romance author. You're more qualified than most people."

A qualified person wouldn't have thought a man

was going to propose to her when really he was gearing up to dump her.

"You're also scheduled for a booksigning at that bookstore café you requested, Grounds for Thought, as well as some stock signings around the Bay Area." Paul handed her another sheet of paper.

"Fine." Grounds for Thought was her friend Eve's café. She hated booksignings, but if she had to do one she might as well support a friend.

Paul pointed a finger at her. "Don't let the promotional things get in the way of writing. They're expecting another bestseller, Lola."

"Aye, aye, captain." She stood up and saluted him. She'd do it, too. She just wasn't sure how.

Paul shook his head. "Wiseass. Get out of my office." He was bent over his desk and working again before she closed the door.

Mary, his assistant, glanced up. "You look fairly unscathed."

"He never leaves visible marks," Lola said as she walked out. Patting her bag to make sure the chapters were there, she hailed a cab and headed from downtown to Laurel Heights, where she lived.

She hadn't been thrilled when she first moved to

Laurel Heights. It wasn't her type of neighborhood. She'd have preferred someplace younger and hipper, like Nopa or the Mission, but Laurel Heights was the most convenient. She'd lucked out in meeting some great people, like Eve and Gwen, the woman who owned the gourd shop downstairs from Lola's apartment. Then there was Olivia and a host of other people who'd made her feel welcome.

The cab driver let her off precisely in front of the address she'd given him. A good tip and a smile, and she hopped out of the car and strode into The Sunrise Care Home.

The scent of Lysol and old people assaulted her as she walked through the doors. She should have been used to the smell by now—she'd been coming here three times a week for the past year—but it still jarred her. It was the smell of sadness, hopelessness, and death, and it always brought tears to her eyes.

Her mother lived here, in it.

By the time she reached her mother's floor, she'd blinked the tears away and had her perma-smile back firmly on her face. She stopped at the nurses' station, needing a moment before going in.

Letty, the day nurse, looked up guiltily from the

book she was reading. "This is your fault," she said, holding up the book.

"I hear that author does great sex scenes."

"My husband thinks so." The nurse leaned in and whispered. "Last night, I read the one on page one hundred twenty-six out loud to him. He was *very* inspired. Thank you, Lola."

She patted Letty's arm. "I'll bring you another book when you finish that one."

"Are you kidding? I've already ordered everything you've written." The nurse sobered. "Sally isn't feeling well today."

"More so than usual?" Lola asked carefully, any levity she was feeling faded.

"It's more than the dementia. She has some congestion. The doctor was worried she was headed toward pneumonia, so he has her on an inhaler." Letty's face was full of compassion. "I just wanted you to have a heads up."

"Thank you." Steeling her shoulders, she strode to her mother's room, took a deep breath, and pushed the door open with a wide smile on her face. "Hi, Mom!"

Sally Carmichael looked up from where she was

knitting in the window seat. She looked pale and tired, not rosy like always. Her forehead furrowed in confusion. "Are you the new housekeeper?"

Lola's heart sank, and the hurt cut deep. She knew it wasn't her mom's fault—dementia was a cruel disease—but the little girl in her was still hurt every time her mom didn't recognize her.

She reaffixed the bright smile on her face and said, "I'm me—Lola. I came to read to you."

Pulling up a chair, she sat down and took out the pages from her purse.

Her mom saw the bound pages and looked curious again. "Oh. Is it a love story?"

"We specialize in love stories here."

"They're my favorite," her mom said, setting aside the knitting.

"I know," Lola said softly. Clearing her throat, she began to read. "'*Louise met him at a party she didn't want to go to. The first thing she thought when she saw Calvin was that he had more hair than a chinchilla.*'"

Lola read on, cringing on the inside as she related the story of how she and Kevin had met, telling herself it was just a story. Louise and Calvin didn't exist.

Lola and Kevin didn't either.

She finished reading the last bit and set the pages aside.

"I love Louise," her mom declared. "She's a wonderful girl."

Lola's heart melted. "Thanks."

"But that Calvin." Sally shook her head. "I don't know about him. He sounds like..."

A self-absorbed prick? "Like what?"

"Not right for Louise."

Lola frowned at the pages. "He seemed right."

"Maybe." Sally sounded doubtful, but then she brightened. "But it's early in the story, so maybe he'll grow and deserve her in the end. Maybe his chin will get stronger."

Unlikely. "I'll see what I can do about that."

"Good. Louise is a lovely girl. She deserves the love of a great man."

Lola swallowed the lump in her throat. "I'll have more for you at the end of the week."

"What day is this? I think I have to take my husband to the doctor." A panicked look came over her mom's face, and then it glazed over into the blankness Lola hated most.

She got up and kissed her mom on her cheek,

briefly so she wouldn't get upset by the familiarity. Sally still smelled like her mother, even if she didn't remember who she was. "See you later, Mom," she said as chipper as she could.

But her mom just sat there, unseeing. Lost.

Lola watched for a moment before quietly letting herself out. She brushed the tears from the corners of her eyes and walked out. Screw sales and best-seller lists—she had to write a kickass romance for her mom.

Chapter Two

SAM PRESSED HIS forehead against the cool surface of the desk, his hands crossed over the back of his skull to keep his head from exploding.

Too much tequila last night. He should've known better than to drink so much. He was frickin' thirty-four years old—he should've had enough common sense by now to know that tequila only made him reckless.

Amanda last night: case in point.

At least he hadn't slept with her. What little common sense he did have prevented that mistake. He shook his head, then moaned and stopped before his brains spilled onto the desk.

Not that he had much in that department, in his opinion. The evidence was stacked against him:

1. At the age of twenty-two, he'd accidentally

gotten his girlfriend Chelsea pregnant on the same night he accepted his first pro-football contract.

2. He'd married Chelsea, because that was what a man did, and they'd had Madison some months later.

3. He'd wrecked his promising football future at twenty-three, by blowing out his knee skiing.

Marriage had been... not good. Whoever said it was better to have loved and lost was a jackass.

He'd had delusions of what love was like, and he tried to live them out with Chelsea. It'd been pointless. She'd loved his potential football stardom more than she'd loved him. When that was gone, so was all pretense of affection.

Fortunately, that horror had ended three years ago. Madison was the only good thing to come from it—the only good thing in his life.

Unfortunately, Chelsea knew he felt that way so she constantly messed with him. Like yesterday, when he was supposed to pick his daughter up to take her out for her birthday—until Chelsea decided

that wasn't convenient for her.

It tore his heart not being with Madison, especially on her birthday. Especially when he'd promised.

The door of his office screeched like it was a crypt gate opening.

He waved a hand blindly over his head. "Go away."

Something dropped onto his desk. "Taylor," a stark feminine voice said.

Just when he thought life couldn't get worse...

Of course, this thing with Jennifer was his fault too. The product of another insanely bad decision. You don't shit where you eat, and you don't screw your boss.

But he had.

"Drink the coffee," she ordered.

Something hot touched his arm. He lifted his head enough to see the mug before him. "Is it poisoned?"

"I wouldn't put you out of your misery that easily."

"True." Gingerly, he sat up and took a sip. It went down hot and soothing, and for a second he was incredibly grateful to Jennifer.

Then she spoke. "What was last night's name? Monica? Jessica?"

Jennifer's voice held an edge that made his head throb harder. But he couldn't blame her—he'd been a jerk to her. Not that he'd made her any promises, but he should have known better than to go there with a woman like her. She wanted hearts and flowers and candles, and he was done with that bullshit.

The only reason he'd gotten personally involved with her was because he'd had too much tequila that night too, and Jennifer had been kind and willing to listen. She'd been warm to hold, and it'd been so long since anyone had been sweet to him...

"Well?" she asked archly, perching primly on the edge of his desk.

"There was only Don Julio," he replied in a croak.

"Obviously you two don't get along." She studied him like he was lower than dirt. "You're pathetic," she finally declared.

No kidding. Thirty-four, a failed marriage, and an eleven-year-old daughter he only got to see when his ex was feeling benevolent. At least his career was going strong.

"I've decided to change your programming," Jennifer said.

He sat up as abruptly as his pounding head would allow. "What?"

"I'm changing your time slot and programming."

He couldn't say anything for a second, he was so taken off balance. "Why? My ratings are solid. Management would never go for that."

"They already have. We need you to bump up ratings for a different segment. I assured management you were the perfect man for the job."

"Which segment?"

"The love hour."

"*No*." He set down the mug with a *clank*, not caring that the hot coffee sloshed onto his hand.

"Yes." The smirk on Jennifer's face was pure evil. "As of Friday night, Touchdown Taylor is going to be Touchy-feely Taylor."

He gaped at her, waiting for her to say she was just jerking him around. God knew he deserved it after the way he'd treated her. Still—this was his career. It was the only way he remained connected to football. It was the way he made sure Madison had everything she needed, from the necessities to therapy so she wouldn't be scalded from the divorce. "I know I wasn't nice to you, Jennifer—"

"You were a bastard," she corrected mildly.

He nodded. "I was a bastard. A total bastard. But this is my career. I can't just change and start doing, what? Relationship counseling?"

"Of course you can't. You don't know what *relationship* means."

"Okay." He relaxed. "So we agree."

"But you *are* going to host *Ladies' Night*, our new segment dedicated to all things love and romance." Her grin was pure satisfaction. "I told management you were the perfect guy for it, what with all your experience with women."

"You're an evil woman."

"I know," she said gleefully, swinging her legs.

"Why are you doing this?"

"Because I like seeing you squirm."

He knew she'd been upset when he hadn't wanted to see her after that one night they'd had, but he hadn't realized she'd been so badly hurt. Part of him was glad she was punishing him this way. He deserved it. "I didn't mean to treat you callously, Jennifer. I regret it if you took it that way."

All the starch dissolved from her and he saw the lovely woman he'd shared that one evening with. "I know, Sam."

"Then why are you doing this?"

"To save you from yourself. To teach you about love."

"Yeah, but *why*? Why would you care? It doesn't make sense."

"Because underneath the arrogant bastard exterior, there's a nice guy, and I think he deserves a chance." She shrugged. "Maybe you remind me of someone. Maybe I don't want another woman to be hurt by you. Maybe my dad was brought down by alcohol. Maybe it's a combination of all that."

"You're crazy."

"Maybe that's part of it too."

He shook his head. "I'm not going to learn about love on the radio."

"You have to, because I'm not letting you go back to your sports talk segment until you do." She hopped off his desk. The clack of her heels on the floor sounded like a time bomb for his career.

"What if I quit?" he called after her.

She looked over her shoulder as she opened the

door. "You can't quit. We own you. You still have three years on your contract. Besides, where would you go, even if you could get out of your contract? New York? Chicago? The only other stations that can afford you are in big cities, and we all know how vested you are in staying in San Francisco."

To be close to Madison. He glared at Jennifer.

She had the grace to look remorseful. "It's for your own good, Sam. You'll see. You start Friday. Your first guest is a local author. Lola Carmichael. She writes romance novels."

"Roman—"

But Jennifer was out the door before he could finish his thought.

Hands at his temples, he leaned back and tried to sort things out in his muzzy head.

Man's man Touchdown Taylor was now hosting a love segment called *Ladies' Night* until his boss decided he was suitably in love with someone. And there wasn't a damn thing he could do about it.

How messed up was that?

One thing he knew for sure: he and Don Julio were definitely never meeting up again.

Chapter Three

HE WALKED INTO Grounds for Thought at precisely 6:15am, just like every morning.

And just like every morning in the few weeks since she started working there, the second Kristin saw him striding toward the counter—toward *her*—the voice inside whispered, *I want him*. Her heart beat faster, her fingers twitched, and something deep and low went all fizzy with excitement. She stood up straight and alert, smiling even though she wasn't a morning person.

It was so strange, because he wasn't her type. Usually she went for techie hipsters—pretty men in skinny jeans.

This man was nothing like the men she'd known before. He wasn't classically beautiful, but he was manly and it turned her on. He oozed sex, and she wanted him to ooze sex all over her.

If only she knew his name. She'd seen him every morning she worked, but she hadn't been able to find a smooth way to introduce herself.

"Hey there," she called out before he reached the counter. "Your usual? Coffee and a scone, to go?"

"Yes, please," he replied, fishing his wallet out of his pocket.

His sleep-husky voice always sent a shiver up her spine. She stared at him, at his strong hands that seemed capable of *everything*, and sighed. He was always dressed impeccably in a suit tailored to fit his marvelous form. Everything about him was neat and deliberate, from the top of his trimmed head to the tip of his polished shoes. And he looked at a person like he could see all the way inside.

She wanted him to do more than see inside her—she wanted him all the way in.

Her female parts tingled in accordance.

Why he turned her on so much, she had no idea. But she knew he was the man to give her what she wanted most in this world: a baby. She could feel her aging eggs cheering her on.

First, his name. After that, she'd ask if he'd donate his sperm to the cause.

"My coffee?" he prompted, holding the money out further.

"How about me instead?"

His brow furrowed. "Excuse me?"

She smiled brightly, mentally chiding herself as she gave him change. "Your coffee, of course."

Knowing he was a stickler for time, she got his order together quickly and handed it to him.

"Thank you," he said. You could tell a lot about people by the way they treated the people who served them, and he was always polite and respectful.

She liked that. She liked him. She leaned her hips against the counter. "You know, you come in every morning and I don't know your name."

"Robert Cray. Rob."

Even his name turned her on. "I'm Kristin," she said, holding out her hand.

His palm slid against hers, an electric tide of sensation. She pulled him closer. What would he do if she kissed him, right there and then?

He'd think she was insane, based on the way he was looking at her. She grinned at herself and let him go. "Nice to meet you, Rob."

He stared at her in a quizzical way. Then he

nodded and left.

She sighed again, watching him stride out the door. She yearned for him.

She yearned for his sperm.

"You're drooling," Eve said, coming around the counter with a tray of hot muffins.

"Can you blame me? The scenery here is mouth-watering."

Eve laughed as she set the tray aside. "I was exactly that way about Treat. He'd come in every morning for a mocha, and I'd want to serve myself up to him instead."

Kristin stared out the window, down the street where Rob had disappeared. She was going to offer herself to him, she decided then and there. She hadn't gotten to where she was by shying away from challenge. "And now look at you. Your wedding is only a few weeks away."

Eve smiled brightly. "It's going to be the event of the year."

"I know. I saw your guest list." Eve had even invited her, and they'd only known each other a short time.

"We wanted everyone to be included. You only

get married once. At least, that's what we're banking on."

"I have no doubt you and Treat will be joined forever," Kristin said, positive to the core. The only other cohesive couple she'd seen was her parents.

She'd always assumed her parents were an anomaly, and all her attempts at relationships had only reinforced that belief, hence her decision to forego the struggle of a partner and just have a child. But now, seeing Eve, she wondered...

She thought of Robert Cray and tried to picture being with him. It wasn't hard. It involved a lot of sex.

There were worse things.

One thing was certain: she'd made a good decision coming to work here. She'd needed to get out and meet people—men, specifically. Staying home and aimlessly fiddling with her computers wasn't going to get her any closer to having a baby. Laurel Heights had seemed like a good neighborhood to meet smart, successful men. "I knew working here was the right decision for me."

"I'm happy to have you." Her boss squeezed her arm. "I may want to hire someone else, too, so if you have friends who're looking let me know."

She laughed, picturing asking the management team at Aspire if they wanted to pull espresso and serve cookies. If they knew their former CEO and founder was doing precisely that, they'd have panicked, wondering if their stock was devaluing.

It wasn't. The company was as healthy as ever. She didn't work with them any longer, in any capacity, but since she still owned a hefty chunk of stock in Aspire she kept track of how it did.

Not that she needed to—she had more money than she knew what to do with. But as much money as she had, she didn't have the one thing she really wanted.

"Call me if you need help out here," Eve said as she headed back to the kitchen.

Kristin waved at her and smiled at another patron. She chatted amiably with the woman as she prepped her latte—skinny, with vanilla syrup.

She loved it at Grounds for Thought. The patrons were nice, she loved Eve, and Eve's friends had taken her into their fold. She felt like she belonged. At Aspire, she'd always been the boss. Here, she was one of the girls.

She liked that. She hadn't been one of the girls

since high school. She was thirty-eight now.

Which meant she didn't have that much time before her window of opportunity for having a child closed. She'd do whatever she had to—even a turkey baster, if that was what it took. But *she* wanted to pick the man who'd father her child. In person, not from a catalog. She wanted to get a feel for him and know that he was smart and kind.

Rob Cray was the one.

It was her own fault that she'd reached this desperate point. From the time she'd dropped out of college she'd been engrossed in building and growing Aspire, a high-end web development company. Now Aspire had offices around the world and was known as the best at what they did.

But the cost had been great. In her twenties, her biological clock had begun ticking. Instead of looking for a guy to mate with, she'd stifled her clock, ignoring its increasingly manic ticking.

Now it was a time bomb, set to self-destruct at any second.

It was completely illogical, driven by a need so deep and elemental that even though she didn't understand it, she couldn't question it.

In her circles, it was completely un-PC to want to be a mom. She'd been groomed to work hard and be a career woman, ruling the world one keystroke at a time. But she was done with that. Her heart told her it was time to move on to the next challenge, and that was being a mother.

It'd be the greatest thing she'd ever do, too. She was going to rock it.

She just needed to get pregnant. With Rob Cray's help, if she had anything to say about it.

Chapter Four

JENNIFER BREEZED INTO the sound booth, looking like the cat that ate the canary. "Are you ready for *Ladies' Night,* Taylor?"

It was only because Sam knew he'd put himself into this situation that he didn't tell her where she could stick her program. Instead he glared at her and went over the lineup one more time. The highlight was Lola Carmichael, a romance novelist.

Jesus H.

Jennifer punched his shoulder. "Don't mess this up, Taylor, or you'll never see sports ever again."

"I love incentives," he said as she walked out.

If only he could be angry with her. Problem was, this was his fault, so all his anger was directed at himself.

His cell phone rang. Fishing it out of his pocket, he answered when he saw it was Madison. "Hey, honey. What's up?"

"I just called to wish you good luck with your new show."

His heart swelled. She'd done that to him constantly since the moment she'd been born. "Thanks. You can't listen."

"Oh, yeah, I can." She lowered her voice. "Steven is over, so she won't notice."

Steven was Chelsea's new boyfriend. Frankly, Sam didn't care what his ex-wife did, except when she did it around his daughter. The guy seemed nice enough, but he wished Chelsea would be more discreet around Madison. Madison was already precocious enough on her own. "Are you in your room?"

"Where else would I be?" There was a pause, and he pictured her rolling her eyes. "So I've been thinking about your new show."

"I wish you wouldn't."

"I have to. You're my dad. Anyway, I think this is a good thing."

"You do," he said flatly.

"Well, yeah. It'll help you get in touch with your feminine side. I love you, but sometimes you're all football and man stuff."

"Have you been watching Oprah?"

She laughed. "Oh, Daddy, you're so retro sometimes."

That probably wasn't a compliment, but he'd take it to hear her laugh. Her laughter was the greatest sound in the world.

"I just want you to be happy, Daddy."

He closed his eyes and breathed. She always did that to him—made him feel that softness right in the middle of his chest. "I'm happy. Don't worry about me, honey."

"I can't help it."

It was moments like this when he worried that the divorce had made her grow up too fast. Sometimes she sounded more sophisticated than he was. A kid wasn't supposed to worry about her parent, right? But how the hell was he supposed to know what a kid sounded like?

She suddenly said, "I hear Mom."

"Go. I love you, Madison."

"Love you too, Daddy!" And the connection ended.

That was it. He had to make this work, even if it meant pandering to lovesick women all week. He tucked his phone in his pocket and studied his program notes.

The door to the sound booth opened, and a blonde with big blue eyes poked her head in. He couldn't see anything below her shoulders, but everything above looked *right*.

"Excuse me, is this *Ladies' Night*?" she asked.

Did the rest of her match that sexy voice? He sat up at attention. "Yeah. I'm the host."

"You?" She looked him up and down.

What? He frowned. "What's wrong with me?"

"Nothing's wrong with you. If I wanted someone to beat up my ex-boyfriend, you're the one I'd call."

It should have been a compliment, but coming from her bowed lips, it sounded more like a slam. Which was damn disappointing, because he really liked the look of her.

"I thought Sam Taylor was a woman," she said.

"I'm all male, sweetheart."

"I can see that." She gave him an all-over, candid appraisal that would've had a lesser man blushing.

Okay, she wasn't immune to him either. That was good.

Although he didn't know why it was good. He

shouldn't have cared one way or the other. If this thing with Jennifer had taught him anything, it was to stay away from women.

He had a feeling that'd be a hard resolve to keep around this blonde. "Look, I have a show to run, so if you tell me who you're looking for I can help you find him."

"I'm looking for you." She stepped inside.

He'd been right—she was *hot*. Tall. Curvy in all the right places and then some. She wore white jeans, a red top, and heels that made her already long legs obscene.

They were the type of legs that men imagined wrapped around their waist.

Sam moved his tongue in his mouth to make sure he hadn't swallowed it.

As if she could read his thoughts, she heaved a sigh. She sounded more exasperated than flattered—and why not? She was the type of gorgeous that probably dealt with men ogling her all the time.

He didn't like that thought.

Then she surprised him by saying, "I'm Lola Carmichael, your guest."

"The romance writer?"

She rolled her eyes. "Duh."

He grinned, liking her spirit. For the first time all day he felt hopeful. Maybe this program was going to be more entertaining than he'd thought. He pointed to the chair across from him. "Please have a seat."

She arched her brows at his polite request. He expected her to make a wise-ass remark, but she surprised him by taking the chair, all calm grace. She looked around the sound studio. "What do I do?"

He gave her a quick rundown, pointing out her microphone and telling her he'd ask a few questions and then they'd take calls. He hoped she couldn't tell how her soapy scent made him want to burrow his face into her skin and inhale her. Or the way he became a blathering idiot every time she focused her blue eyes on him.

There was a knock on the door. It opened to reveal a gloating Jennifer again. "Are we all set?"

"This is Jennifer Simmons, the program manager," Sam explained, leaving out some of the other titles he'd given her this past week. "Jennifer, Lola Carmichael."

Jennifer came in and shook Lola's hand. "Lola, I'm a big fan of your books. I loved the end of *Time*

After Time, when Jesse kidnapped Sarah and held her hostage until he convinced her he really did love her."

Seriously? Sharkie Jennifer, in her conservative suits, was a romance reader? He shook his head, not because he didn't believe it, but because he hadn't known it and he'd been intimate with the woman. She was right—he really was a jerk.

Lola smiled warmly. "I loved writing that scene. Too bad guys aren't really like that, huh?"

They both looked at him like he was lacking. He knew they were right, but still. "Hey. I resent that remark."

Jennifer made a derisive noise, but Lola couldn't hide her grin.

"I'll leave you two at it." Jennifer gave him a death stare. "Don't screw this up."

"Thanks for the pep talk," he called after her.

Lola leaned back in her seat, arms crossed. "Did you guys date before?"

"Why would you ask that?"

"Because she's angry at you for more than taking the last candy bar from the lounge vending machine."

As if he didn't feel bad enough about the situation. "How can you tell?"

"I build characters." She shrugged. "Some things are obvious. Like it's obvious you're a stereotypical playboy."

"What the hell does that mean?"

"You go through women without any regard for their feelings. You make them feel like they're the center of your world, get them to believe you want to spend forever with them, and then you dump them and move on."

He didn't know how to react. Should he be indignant or ashamed? One thing was sure: she'd hit a little too close to home. "And writing pulp teaches you this?"

"My books *rock*," she said proudly. "I may not write the Great American Novel, but people enjoy my books. I write for entertainment, just like Shakespeare."

"I hear they can train monkeys to produce Shakespeare."

Her stunning eyes narrowed, and she leaned forward. "You are a cretin."

"We're on in thirty," he said, knowing that if he grinned she'd really get pissed. He couldn't help it—he felt energized and alive, which was shocking after

dreading the new program all week. He put on his headphones. "Speak into your mic, and this will be over soon."

"That's what *she* said." She adjusted her seat closer to the console.

"Welcome to *Ladies' Night,*" he managed to say without gagging. "I'm your host, Touchdown Taylor—"

"Touchdown?" Lola repeated incredulously.

Only she said it right into her microphone, just like he'd instructed. He frowned at her. "And this is Lola Carmichael, writer of bodice rippers, friend of Fabio, and our guest for tonight's show."

"Thank you, *Touchdown.*" She stuck her tongue out at him.

God save him from high-and-mighty women. "It was a college nickname."

"It's just if you're hosting *Ladies' Night,* maybe you'll want a different nickname. Touchdown gives the wrong impression. Unless you score a lot." She leaned into the microphone. "Don't you think so, ladies?"

He pulled her microphone away from her. "We're here to find out about you, Ms. Carmichael, not to talk about me."

She grabbed the microphone back. "But I'm sure your audience wants to get to know you too. Isn't this your first show?"

"For *Ladies' Night*? Yes."

"So what's a macho man like you doing in a place like this?"

He had the urge to shake her—or push her down and kiss her to shut her up.

Before he could reply, she turned her husky voice into the microphone and said, "It's too bad you can't see him, ladies. He's just like a hero from one of my novels. Tall, dark, and handsome. His hair is mussed up enough to be sexy without being unkempt, and he has those broad shoulders that make all of us sigh in lust."

He only wanted one woman to sigh in lust, and she was seated across from him.

"He has a strong chin too." She looked at him thoughtfully, but then she shook her head. "I'm telling you, he's wasted in radio."

"And you?"

She blinked at him, suspicious. "Me?"

"You don't look like any writer I've ever seen."

"And how many romance writers have you seen?"

Actually, none. "Danielle Steele lives in San Francisco. You don't look like her."

"Of course not. She's old enough to be my mother." Lola wrinkled her nose. "So what do I look like?"

Like his own personal heaven and hell. "Like a showgirl, yellow feathers in your hair and a dress cut down to there."

She leaned forward and pointed a threatening finger at him. "Do *not* quote Barry Manilow to me."

He grinned, wondering if he could find that track to play sometime in the next hour. "Is Lola Carmichael your real name?"

"Yes, Lola Carmichael is my real name."

He could tell it was a sore subject for her by the way her eyes went both icy and hot. He felt bad for poking her in a soft spot so he changed the subject. "Tell us about your latest book, *Here and Forever*."

For a moment he didn't think she'd reply, but then she said, "It's the story of a man and woman who are rivals for the same job, but in their competition find love."

Sam snorted.

"What?" She frowned at him.

"Who got the job?"

"What does that matter?"

"No guy is going to hook up with a woman who wins out over him."

Lola stuck her pretty nose in the air. "That's not true."

"Yeah, it is. You might as well cut his balls off. But then I doubt you write about real men."

"I do, too."

"Sure, sweetheart, whatever you say. They probably bring flowers and candy in order to woo women," he said scornfully.

"What's wrong with that?"

"It's bull"—he cleared his throat and pulled back—"it's *hokey,* is what it is. You're giving women a false sense of reality."

"I write about romance and true love. That's real."

"Right." She looked like she might leap across the table and strangle him, so he turned to his mic. "Let's take some callers and see what they think. On line one, we have Gina from Berkeley. Hello, Gina."

"Hi Gina," Lola echoed brightly as she shot him an evil look.

"Lola, oh my God, I can't believe I'm actually talking to you. This is so awesome. I've read all your

books, and I'm a huge fan."

"Gina, you obviously have excellent taste."

Sam would have thought Lola was being serious if he hadn't seen the self-deprecating smile on her face.

"When is your next book coming out, Lola? And who's starring in it? I hope it's Louise." Gina sighed. "I've been waiting for Louise to find her soul mate forever."

"Haven't we all?" Lola muttered. But into the mic she said, "It's Louise this time, Gina. I think you'll like the story a lot."

Sam frowned. She didn't sound convinced about that. He wanted to point it out, but the look on her face bordered on miserable. For some reason, he didn't have the heart.

So much for hard-hitting Touchdown Taylor. Shaking his head, he said, "Thanks, Gina. Our next caller is Jessica from Walnut Creek. Welcome, Jessica."

"Lola, is Sam really as hot as you described?"

Smirking, Lola gave him a slow once-over. "If you're into the Neanderthal type, he's as good as it gets."

Jessica gave a lusty sigh over the line. "Sam, are you single? Because I think I could rock your world."

"Thanks for calling, Jessica," he said quickly over Lola's laughter. "Next we've got Mike from San Jose. Mike?"

"I had to call in, Touchdown," the gravelly voice said. "Dude, what's this love crap you're talking about? When are you going back to what really counts?"

"Some people think love *is* what really counts, Mike," Lola said mildly.

Both he and Mike scoffed.

Lola pointed at him. "Love is the most important thing in the world. That's why I write romance, to give people hope and to remind them that it's possible to find happiness."

"Sweetheart, you're profiting off people by selling them a fantasy that doesn't exist."

"How dare you? I don't care about profits." She sat up, her cheeks flushed.

She'd look like that while making love, but he didn't need to dwell on that—at all. He shifted his legs, trying to distract the part of him that *did* want to dwell on it. "Of course you care about profits. You

wouldn't do this if you didn't make money."

"Yes, I would."

For some reason, he believed that she actually meant that. "Then you're doubly delusional, for lying to people as well as yourself."

"I'm not lying to anyone."

"About soul mates?" he said, spitting the words out.

"Soul mates exist," she insisted. "My parents were soul mates."

"Do you have a soul mate?"

She recoiled as if he'd slapped her.

He instantly regretted putting that pained look in her eyes. It was on the tip of his tongue to apologize when she said, "It's obvious your idea of a soul mate is someone who'll fetch your slippers for you."

The regret evaporated. "Nah. I'd rather her fetch me a beer and the remote."

Lola leaned toward him. "Did I mention you're a cretin?"

"Yes, and I'm sure you will again."

The caller cleared his throat. "Um, guys, wouldn't it just be better to get a room?"

"No," he and Lola exclaimed at once. They glared at each other as he patched through the next caller

without looking at the information. "Hello"—he looked at the ID—"*Madison*?"

"Hi, Daddy."

Lola whirled in her chair to face him, brows arched in question.

He shook his head. "Madison, this show isn't appropriate for you."

"I know, but I'm eleven so you know I'm going to rebel. Besides, I have a question for Lola."

Lola chuckled softly. "Go ahead, Madison."

"Do your books have lots of sex in them?"

Jesus H. Sam waved manically at Lola.

Lola winked at him devilishly and then said, "Yes, there's a fair bit of sex in my books. If you're eleven, I'm not sure they'd be appropriate for you, but that's for your parents to decide. Do you like to read?"

"Yeah. I read a lot of different things."

"But you're not reading Lola's books," Sam interjected.

Madison gave the kind of exasperated sigh only an eleven year old could. "*Daddy*."

"Goodnight, honey." He hung up, shaking his head. God, he loved that kid, even when she tested him.

But he didn't want her head filled with nonsense about true love and soul mates. He'd worked hard to keep that Disney princess crap from infecting her. He wanted his daughter to be strong and independent, not someone who needed to be saved or who believed in fairy tales.

Lola watched him. He could practically see the wheels churning in her head.

He didn't like it. It was like she was measuring him—like she could see into him—and he didn't need Ms. Romance going there. So he said, "Where do you get your inspiration? Where do the ideas for your characters come from?"

She rolled her eyes, but when she answered, it was gracefully. "From life. People I know, people I meet."

He snorted. "Manly paragons like the ones you write about don't exist."

"Have you read my books?"

"Enough to know what I'm talking about." He'd read the excerpt that was in the press packet.

"I suppose your idea of a real man is one who grunts and scratches himself in public."

"My idea of a real man is one who takes care of

his responsibilities and protects the people he cares about."

She blinked. "Well, I can't argue with that, can I?"

"A smart man would end the show on that note, and my momma didn't raise no dummy." He cued the awful theme music. "Thanks for joining us, and until next time I'm Touch—Sam Taylor with *Ladies' Night*."

Chapter Five

As soon as the sappy theme music came on, Lola shoved the microphone away. She should have felt irritated and upset, but, truthfully, she felt exhilarated. She hadn't felt so alive in forever.

She knew it was partly because he looked like one of her heroes come to life. She hadn't been exaggerating when she described him to that caller: Sam Taylor was knee-weakening, panty-dampening *hot*.

Not that she was going to let him know she thought that. So she stood and glared at him. "Is that how you treat all your guests?"

He shrugged. "Yeah."

"You're a jerk."

"Was that in question?" He stood up, dropped his headphones on the console, and reached out a hand. "Thanks for coming by. Good luck with your book."

The *book*. She groaned. She didn't hype it the way

she was supposed to. Paul and her publisher weren't going to be happy. "You didn't let me talk about my book!"

"Sure I did." Shrugging, he lowered his hand. "You chose to attack me instead."

"I didn't attack you." She punched him in the arm.

He didn't even flinch.

She knew the way these macho types worked—she wrote about them, after all. "Don't think that by standing there and looking hot you can get away with being a jerk."

"You think I'm hot?"

"Well, I'm not blind."

He stepped closer to her. He didn't touch her, but she felt him all over. "You're not bad either."

What was she talking about? Oh, yeah. "The interview was a mess. You barely asked me any relevant questions."

"That's not true, sweetheart."

He said the endearment like a soft caress, and she shivered at the feel of it. "Don't try to distract me."

"Trust me, sweetheart, if I were trying to distract you, you'd definitely know it."

She snorted. She believed him, but he didn't need to know that. He was cocky enough as it was. "So how did Touchdown Taylor end up hosting a love line for women?"

His face was suddenly shuttered. "The execs thought I'd raise the ratings."

Ah—it had to do with Jennifer. She almost felt sorry for him. He was an idiot—what man wasn't?—but after hearing him talk with his daughter, she knew he wasn't cruel. So she said, "Your execs must be smoking crack."

The spark came back into his eyes. "Careful."

For some reason, she didn't want to be careful. She felt reckless, like she wanted to poke at the lion. "I bet this is like time-out for you. What did you do? Come in to work late? Piss off the wrong person?"

He reached out and hauled her into his chest, his mouth on hers before his arms were around her.

The kiss was urgent.

Physical.

All-encompassing.

His hands clenched her to him, and for the first time ever it felt just like how she wrote about it. Her toes even curled.

He lifted her from her butt. Without thought, she anchored her legs around his hips and grabbed his hair.

Whirling around, he pressed her to the wall. She was surprised that he took care not to slam her. Then the only thing she was aware of was the insistent ridge of his hard-on against the vee of her legs.

It felt *good*. She wanted to feel more, with less layers of clothing.

His hands slid up under her shirt—

And then her phone rang, the nuclear alarm ring tone she'd assigned to Kevin after he'd broken up with her. He called constantly, even though she never answered. She'd like to think he was desperate to get back together, but she suspected his insistent phone calls had more to do with him being desperate to reunite with his favorite T-shirt, which still resided in her closet.

She broke the kiss. Panting, she looked around. They were one step away from getting it on in a sound room without locking the door. "Stop."

He let her go like a hot potato.

She caught her balance on the wall, glaring at him. He didn't have to be so eager about it. "Do you molest all your guests?"

"Historically, my guests have had no necks and were covered in hair. So, no." He raked his hand through his hair. "And I didn't molest you. You molested me."

"You wish." She grabbed her purse and shot him one more glare. "You are a cretin."

"You said that already. Twice."

"Well, I'm reaffirming it. See you never." She lifted her head and marched out, aware of him watching her leave. She put an extra swish in her hips, just so he knew what he was missing out on.

When the door closed behind her, she slumped against the first wall. "Oh. My. God," she muttered, shaking her head to clear the still present drunkenness his kiss caused.

Sam "Touchdown" Taylor was dangerous. Good thing she was never seeing him again. She'd already trusted one selfish man with her heart—she wasn't foolish enough to repeat that mistake.

Chapter Six

KRISTIN KNEELED ON her hands and knees and made kissy sounds.

There wasn't the faintest hint of response from behind the trash cans, even though she'd seen the puppy duck behind there, skittish, when she'd brought the garbage out.

It was the fourth sighting she'd had in the past week. The poor thing looked thin and bedraggled—not like the pampered Laurel Heights pooches with manicured paws and little sweaters. She felt so sorry for it, instead of going home after work, she'd come out here to look for it.

A stray? Abandoned? She didn't know because she couldn't get close enough to check for a collar. He ran away every time she got close.

Yesterday she had the brilliant idea to lure him out with food, so she'd stopped at the *chi-chi* pet boutique down the street and bought organic, home-made dog food. What starved creature could resist a handout, much less a gourmet one?

Kristin opened the bag and smelled it. Good, actually. She popped a small piece in her mouth and chewed. She had two older brothers—she'd eaten worse things in her life.

And the puppy food wasn't half bad. She sprinkled a line of it out from the garbage cans to a foot away from where she crouched. Then she made more kissy sounds, wiggling her butt for good measure. Dogs did it—it must have meaning in canine vocabulary. "Come on, big boy. I've got something here that you want."

"What, precisely, is that?" a deep voice said from directly behind her.

Startled, she tried to spin around but fell on her butt instead.

Rob Cray stood above her. He didn't look as kempt as he did in the mornings. His tie was missing, and his shirt was unbuttoned at the collar. His normally impeccable hair was rumpled, as if he'd run his hands through it countless times. Had he had a hard day? She had the urge to embrace him and press a kiss to his neck to wipe away the stress.

He looked at the bag in her hand. "Are you eating dog food?"

"It's tasty." She smiled brightly to cover up feeling awkward. Standing, she brushed her hands off on her pants. "But, really, I'm looking for the dog."

"Is that some sort of euphemism?"

She laughed. "No, there's a puppy who's been hanging around the garbage cans. I was worried about him, so I bought him some food from the store down the street to try to get him to trust me."

He frowned at the bag.

"It's good stuff," she assured him. "It was more expensive than groceries for a week."

His frown deepened, but as he started to talk, she heard a rustling sound.

She turned around and saw the little thing poke its head out. It had large dark eyes, one ear that stood up, and a white face. "Aren't you adorable?" she cooed, going back to her knees. "Come here, little guy. I won't hurt you."

Apparently, he didn't believe her because he ducked back behind the trash.

"You're out here in the dark, playing with a puppy?" Rob said.

She shook her head. "I'm rescuing him."

"Is that what this is called?"

She rolled her eyes. "You're just cranky because you had a hard day."

"How do you know?"

"It's totally obvious. And you're coming home late."

"You keep track of when I come home?"

"Don't make it sound like I'm a stalker. I'm just observant. When I work the afternoon shift, I notice you come home before I leave for the day, around six. It's"—she looked at the time—"almost eight now."

"If you go home around six, what are you doing here?"

"You're so suspicious." Shaking her head, she stood up again. She'd been setting up the new iPad cash register system for Eve. It hadn't taken long, except that she'd added a few customized pieces that she thought Eve would enjoy. "I worked late, too. And then I saw the dog, so I've been out here a while trying to coax him out."

The dog poked its nose out again.

Rob frowned at the dog and then said, "Dog, sit."

The puppy immediately sat its butt on the ground,

eyes wide and alert.

"How did you do that?" Kristin asked, indignant.

He took the bag of dog food from her hand, scooped a handful, and knelt down. "Come," he told the dog as he held his hand out.

She shook her head. "I don't think he'll—"

The puppy lunged forward, eagerly munching the food straight from Rob's hand.

"Amazing." She looked at Rob, impressed. "He likes you."

"She. Look at her undercarriage."

Kristin peeked under the dog. "Oh. Well, no wonder."

"What?"

"It makes sense that you'd have a female eating out of your hands, regardless of the species."

He turned away, but not before she saw the quirk of a smile at his lips. "Do you have water?"

"No, but I can get some. Or we can go inside," she said as a cold breeze swept through. She hugged her arms around her.

"Where's your coat?" he asked with a frown.

She wrinkled her nose as she thought about it. "I think in the hall closet in my apartment." She'd been plotting out a way to ask Rob to be her sperm donor when she left her place that morning, and then she started thinking so deeply she became tunnel-visioned. A coat had been the last thing on her mind, especially when her thoughts had been occupied with Rob keeping her warm.

Standing, Rob took his coat off and wrapped it around her. He closed it tight and shook his head. "You have no sense whatsoever, do you?"

"Sure I do. This was in my plans all along. If I had a coat you'd never be right here, would you?" She grinned and snuggled closer to him.

"You're crazy."

"I must be, to do this." She pulled his head down and kissed him.

Delicious. Warm, dark, and rich, like one of Eve's chocolate croissants fresh from the oven. Kristin loved chocolate croissants.

She loved this kiss even more.

Him, a voice inside her insisted. Being this close put her girl parts into overdrive. Her eggs were standing up and cheering her along. Humming in pleasure, she pressed closer and wrapped her arms around his neck.

She'd never been so aggressive before. In her experience, men liked to be the conquerors. But this was thrilling. She was in control—in charge of her own destiny.

If she'd wanted a relationship with him, she'd have lured him more slowly instead of hitting him over the head and dragging him to her. But she just wanted to hook up. A couple weeks of sex ought to do it. She was near ovulation.

Rob didn't push her away. In fact, she felt *his* bits stir against her. Only calling them *bits* was a big injustice—*big* being the operative word.

"Stop it." His hands gripped her waist and held her off. "We don't know each other."

"I'm proposing we get to know each other."

"We shouldn't be out here doing this," he said.

"You're right. Take me home."

He shook his head, but there was a smile flirting with his lips. "You don't give up, do you?"

"Not when I know what I want."

He stared at her like he was seeing her for the first time. His gaze dropped to her mouth, as though he was contemplating kissing her again.

She wanted it—badly. But she knew that if she

initiated it this time, she'd be pushing him away. It was clear he liked things by the book, and she'd already disrupted his world with her brazenness.

As if agreeing with her thoughts, the puppy barked once.

"We should take her in." Kristin sighed and stepped away. "She's cold."

Rob stared at her a moment longer, as if he wasn't sure what to make of her, before scooping the animal into his arms. The puppy snuggled there happily, like she belonged with him.

Kristin made a face at the beast. "Flirt."

Rob looked at her like she was insane, but she shook her head. "I get it," she said. "You're taking another woman home with you tonight. But I'm not letting this go."

He shook his head. "No. *No,* I'm not taking this dog home. And there's nothing to let go here."

"You have to take the dog. Pets are forbidden in my lease, and we can't leave her outside. She'll freeze to death."

As if knowing they were discussing her fate, the dog looked up at him imploringly.

Kristin smiled at it. She couldn't fault the puppy

for trying to go home with Rob. "Look, Chanel loves you already."

"Chanel?"

Covering the dog's ears, she leaned in and whispered, "If she's going to live in this neighborhood, she needs a name that'll give her a little class, at least until she gets a makeover and new wardrobe."

"Don't name the dog, for God's sake," he said.

"Too late, isn't it, Chanel?" Kristin scratched behind the one floppy ear, and the puppy wriggled happily.

"Damn it," Rob muttered, looking down at them helplessly.

Kristin grinned. "I'd take her home but, like I said, I can't have pets. Plus, she's picked you anyway. At least you won't have to worry about food. You can have this bag."

"That's generous of you," he said with an edge of sarcasm.

"I know." She smiled blithely. Standing on her toes, she kissed him one last time, to make sure the first time wasn't a fluke.

It wasn't. At all.

Sex was going to be *so good*.

Sighing, she smiled at him. "We'll do that more next time."

"There won't be a next time."

"Yes, there will." She frowned, troubled by a sudden thought. "Unless you're taken."

"Of course I'm not." He glared at her. "I'd never cheat on someone I was seeing."

Relieved, she smiled again. "Good. Then it's a date."

"No, it's not."

She waved over her shoulder. "Dream of me tonight, Rob. I'll definitely be dreaming of you, and I can tell you, you won't be wearing anything more than my naked body."

He issued a string of curses behind her.

She laughed, happy. Excited. Eager. She'd found her baby daddy.

Chapter Seven

Louise was watching Calvin chew his steak, his mouth occasionally smacking open, when she noticed the tall, dark cowboy across the room. He looked like a vigilante, a bad boy with a heart of gold, and she caught herself looking to see if he had a white hat hidden somewhere.

Next to the cowboy, Calvin looked weak. Especially in the chin.

She had an urge to smack him across that weak chin, too. Before she gave in to the urge, she excused herself and went to the restroom.

The cowboy was there, waiting for her.

Her heart skipped a beat, and she caught herself sauntering over to him.

"Hey, girl," he drawled, reaching out to her as she approached. He speared his hand into her long blond hair and brought her to him—brought her mouth directly to his.

And Louise knew she'd died and gone to heaven...

DELETE.

Whimpering, Lola dropped her head on her keyboard. She couldn't have Louise make out with a mysterious cowboy with Calvin in the other room, even if Calvin *was* a jerk.

Her problem was that she couldn't stop thinking about the kiss Sam had forced on her. She'd never admit it to anyone, especially not Sam, but that kiss had rocked her world.

She needed fresh air, otherwise she'd never get anywhere with this chapter. Closing her laptop, she got up, put on flip-flops, and headed to Outta My Gourd, her friend Gwen's shop.

In short, Gwendolyn Pierce was odd. She did amazingly well as a gourd artist and owned her own store. Moreover, a couple months earlier they'd all found out Gwen was really Genevieve de la Roche, a runaway heiress. Gwen had refused to go back to her former life though. She was still Gwen, she still owned her gourd gallery, and she'd recently gotten involved with one good-looking private investigator.

Lola walked into Gwen's store. As usual, no one was up front, but Gwen bustled from her workshop

in the back as soon as she heard the front door. And, also as usual, her friend lit up when she saw Lola. "Hey! I heard your interview last night."

Lola groaned. "Please let's not talk about it."

"It was fabulous." Gwen grinned. "You and the DJ had sparks."

"No, we didn't. He was a cretin."

"A cretin who pushed your buttons."

"There was no button pushing," she lied.

"If you say so." Gwen didn't look like she believed her though. "So how's the book coming along?"

"I don't want to talk about that either."

Gwen arched a brow. "Do we need to take a break and have some girl time?"

"Are you going to interrogate me?"

"Yes, but I promise I won't use the methods Rick uses on me." She grinned impishly, blushing ever so slightly.

The romantic in Lola sighed. Gwen and Rick were a fairy tale come to life. Gwen had been harboring a secret, and Rick had been determined to uncover it. They'd overcome everything and were blissful now.

The recent cynic in Lola pouted. She couldn't

find fault with them as a couple, and that was discouraging on a personal level.

"What's wrong with you? You're usually disgustingly bright-eyed, but you look like someone burst your balloon."

"Burst my bubble," she corrected. "I'm just having a hard time writing. I need a break."

Gasping in alarm, Gwen walked right up to her and put her hand on Lola's forehead. "When do you ever have a hard time writing? Do you have a fever?"

"Not unless being hot and bothered by a jerk counts."

"Did Kevin call you again?"

"Yes, but I didn't answer." He'd left a message though. She'd been right—he wanted his Def Leppard T-shirt back, which she was going to keep, of course. She'd just tuck it deep in her closet so she'd never see it. "But that's not who I'm hot and bothered about."

Gwen gasped again. "The radio guy!"

Lola thought about the kiss and melted all over again.

"You *like* him," her friend shrieked. "Does he like you?"

"You heard us on the radio."

"Then the answer is yes. What's his name? I'll have Rick run a check on him."

"Gwen."

"Seriously. It's what Rick does." She went to flip the lights off. "But for now we're going to Olivia's."

"What for?"

"Lingerie. If Rick okays this guy, you need to be ready."

She dug her heels in as Gwen tried to drag her to the door. "No, I don't."

"You really do. You're a romance writer. You're supposed to be into that sort of frippery."

"Frippery?"

"Romance. Lacy things." Gwen waved her hand dismissively as she locked up. "Whatever."

Lola wasn't sure she needed lacy things, but she could definitely use a little romance to inspire her through this rough spot in her book. However, she didn't need romance with an arrogant radio host who had an eleven-year-old daughter.

But the kiss...

Sighing, she let Gwen drag her over to Romantic Notions, their friend Olivia's lingerie store down the street. Olivia looked up when they walked in, and her shopkeeper's smile brightened when she saw it was them.

Olivia was striking, but when she smiled she was stunning. Now that her pregnancy had started to show, she was especially alluring. On top of that, she was an astute businesswoman and genuinely a good person.

Gwen marched up to Olivia and said, "We need stuff meant to seduce."

"I'm not doing any seducing," Lola said, shaking her head vehemently, even though her girl parts cheered at the idea of getting it on with Sam.

Olivia glanced between the two of them. Then, to Lola's surprise, she said, "I listened to your interview on the radio."

Groaning, Lola dropped her head in her hands.

Olivia laughed. "It was entertaining. I loved the banter between the two of you. No wonder you want lingerie."

"I don't want lingerie." She pointed at Gwen. "*She's* the instigator."

Gwen patted her arm. "You can thank me later."

"I have just the thing for you, Gwen." Becoming

all business, Olivia headed toward a table in front. "Rick is going to love this on you."

Gwen looked at the fuchsia bra set, eyes wide. "There are no cups."

"I know. Go try it on." Olivia turned to Lola. "You."

She blinked. "Me?"

"I have the perfect thing for you, too, but it'd be only for you, not because you want to please someone else."

"What is it?" Lola asked despite herself.

Without a word, Olivia went to the back and came out with a white lace set.

It looked unassuming. It was white and lacy, so nondescript and innocent looking that Lola stared at it doubtfully.

Olivia smiled. "Trust me. Take it home and if it doesn't work out, bring it back."

She wasn't convinced that she needed lingerie but she acquiesced. She was watching Olivia wrap the underwear in burgundy tissue when Gwen skipped out of the dressing room, her cheeks rosy. "Rick's going to love this," she said. "You're right."

"I know," Olivia replied with a coy smile.

The front door opened, and Eve walked in carrying a to-go cup in her hand. "Delivery for the mama-to-be. Decaf Nutella latte, as big as they come."

Moaning, Olivia held her hands out eagerly. "You're my hero. This baby has more of a hazelnut fetish than I do."

"How *is* junior in there?" Gwen asked.

"Enthusiastic." Olivia ran a hand over the small mound of her belly. "He has his father's energy."

"How are you going to run the store once the baby is born?" Lola asked.

"I found a woman to work for me. She starts in a couple weeks. Business is good, and then I can focus on merchandising and being a mom." She nodded at Eve. "You'll like Nicole. She's looking for an apartment, so if you hear of anything let me know."

"It's too bad I just rented out my old apartment," Eve said.

Olivia grinned as she lifted her beverage. "You finally gave up your bachelorette pad, huh?"

"You should see the guy who rented it." Eve leered as best as an angelic looking blonde could. "If I didn't have Treat, I'd be taking him cookies every day."

"Cute?" Gwen asked.

"No. *Hot*."

Gwen nudged Lola. "Maybe *he's* your inspiration."

"I don't think so." Lola had Sam firmly fixed in her head, for some annoying reason.

"He's mysterious too," Eve added. "Kristin, Allison, and I have been conjecturing about what he does. Allison and I think he's a former CIA agent who's on leave, but Kristin believes he's an undercover rock star." She perked up, suddenly excited. "Speaking of additions to the neighborhood, guess who's moving to the neighborhood?"

"Daniela Rossi," Olivia said.

Eve wilted, crestfallen. "How did you know?"

Olivia just arched her brow.

"I should know better than to ask." Eve rolled her eyes. "Anyway, she's moving into Margaret's old teahouse. The rumor is she's opening a custom dessert boutique."

Lola looked back and forth between the women, feeling like she didn't have the whole story. "Who's Margaret? And who's Daniela Rossi?"

"Margaret is Eve's future mother-in-law," Olivia explained.

Eve nodded. "And Daniela is my idol and the reason Grounds for Thought has been so successful as a café bookstore. The booksigning event she did with me really launched the business."

"My booksigning is tomorrow." Lola made a face.

"I know!" Eve enthused. "It's going to be fun. I have your book displayed all over, and I'm making mini lemon tarts for treats. Don't worry about a thing. You'll have a good time. Just come and enjoy it."

Especially if it was going to be her last time, because she wasn't entirely certain the current book was ever going to get off the ground. She thought about what she'd written today and winced.

Crap—everything she'd written in the past month had been pure crap. She hated letting Kevin affect her that way, but he'd derailed her.

If she were smart, she'd write about a different couple, regardless of the fact that her fans expected Louise's story. Fans could be appeased as long as they were given a good story.

The only person who wouldn't be appeased was her mom. Her mom really wanted Louise's story, too. The irony wasn't lost on Lola. Sally couldn't remem-

ber her own daughter's name, but she remembered everything about Louise.

In a way, it was nice. At least her mom was indirectly interested in Lola's life.

Which was why she had to buck up and write the story—for her mom. It was the only way they could stay connected. And her mom believed ardently in fairy tale love. It was the one thing Lola could give her: stories of soul mates.

She had imagination. She could make it up, even if she was beginning to doubt it really existed. After all, even her parents' fairy tale love ended when her dad died.

Gwen nudged her. "You okay?" she asked softly, her large eyes warm with concern.

Lola squeezed her arm. "I will be, once I finish the first draft of this book."

Her friend didn't look like she believed her. Not that she blamed Gwen—she didn't believe herself either.

Chapter Eight

Sam couldn't get Lola out of his head. He couldn't stop thinking about that kiss.

"Isn't the bookstore café to the right?" Madison asked, pointing out the window. "Right there. Grounds for Thought."

"Oh. Yeah." He made a quick series of turns and parked a couple streets away.

Madison barely waited until the car had stopped to jump out. Sam slammed the door shut—hard—hoping the action would close the door on his thoughts of Lola.

No such luck, because he still saw her blue eyes, still felt her long legs wrapped around his waist, and still felt the way her mouth ate at his.

Like she was starving.

"Come on, Daddy." His daughter took his hand and pulled. "We're going to be late."

"Late?" He frowned. For the first time since he'd picked her up that morning, he realized she was up to something more than stopping at the bookstore to pick up a book. "What are we late for?"

"You'll see." She grinned at him with that adorable gap on the left side of her mouth, where her last baby tooth had finally fallen out. "And then I'll be your favorite child."

"You're already my favorite, and do I need to point out you're my only child?"

"Yeah, but one day you'll give me a little brother or sister."

The picture that sprang into his mind was holding Lola and a baby that had her big blue eyes. He frowned. "That seems unlikely."

Madison didn't say anything, focused instead on the store. She was literally bouncing up and down, dragging him down the street behind her. "Come on, Daddy."

"I love that you're excited for this book, honey, but—" His mouth snapped closed as he saw the huge poster advertising a booksigning going on right then, for a book that was just released. *Here and Now* by Lola Carmichael.

He stopped short and stared silently at his daughter.

Instead of looking remorseful, Madison got that stubborn look on her face that he recognized from his own reflection. "You were the one cyber-stalking her," his daughter pointed out.

"I was not."

"Yeah-huh. I saw on your browser."

"I was researching her. For another show," he lied.

Madison rolled her eyes, let go of his hand, and marched right in.

Jesus H. He rushed after her. No telling what the kid would say unsupervised. He caught up to her and took her hand again. "I'm going to put a leash on you."

"Sure, Daddy."

"And a muzzle."

His daughter just beamed the confident smile of a child secure in her father's love.

And then he saw Lola.

She sat at a large table piled with books. There was an impressively long line of people waiting for her. She smiled brightly at the woman standing in front of her and handed her a copy she'd presumably already signed.

But even here, in a bookstore, signing books for fans, she still didn't match his image of an author. She looked like a classy showgirl with her sparkly pink top and flowing hair.

When Madison tugged his hand, he realized he'd unconsciously started to walk slower, savoring the vision of Lola with each step. "Madison, did I mention you're grounded for the rest of your life?"

"If I get a little brother, I'm okay with that." With singleness of purpose, she dragged him to the table.

Ten feet away, Lola looked up, her eyes widening when she saw him. The blush that stained her cheeks told him that she was also remembering their kiss.

Suddenly he wasn't as reluctant to see her. In fact, for the first time in years, he felt that initial rush he used to get before a show when he'd first started in radio, the same kind of adrenaline surge he'd gotten before a football game, back in the day.

Showing the casual disregard that only a kid on the verge of adolescence could exhibit, Madison marched them up to the front of the line and held her free hand out. "I'm Madison Taylor. We talked on the

radio a couple days ago."

"We did," Lola said, giving him a questioning look before she turned all her attention to his daughter. "This is a surprise."

"We're here to buy your book. For my dad."

"We are?" he said.

Madison shot him a withering look before she smiled again at Lola. "He's your biggest fan. He can't wait to read it."

"Really." Lola arched a brow at him. Then she pulled a short stack of novels and began signing them. "Then I'm sure he'll want more than one copy."

What the hell was he going to do with six copies of a romance novel? Pass them out to the boys at poker night? "Madison, forget grounding. You've moved up to a life sentence."

"Daddy doesn't mean it," his daughter assured Lola. "He may be like a guy and talk tough, but he's only ever thought about swatting my butt once, and just the thought made him cry."

He tugged Madison's ponytail. "It's making me pretty gleeful at the moment."

His daughter grinned at him and cuddled into his side. He ran his hand down her soft hair, already feeling how this would all change soon. In a couple years, she'd be a teenager and not want anything to do with him.

Lola stared back and forth at them like she was trying to figure something out. Then she shook her head and shoved the books at him. "You can pay for them at the counter."

"Awesome," Madison exclaimed. "I can't wait to read it."

"You aren't," he and Lola said at once. They stared at each other, confounded by the connection.

"Lola, my dad's taking me to get a hamburger after."

"I am?" he asked.

His daughter ignored him, focusing all her cuteness on the author. "Would you like to come? We'll wait for you," she added, dragging him away before Lola could say anything.

He let her take him to the register. "Madison, I'm not sure what you're up to, but I don't like it."

She made a noncommittal noise.

"What if Lola didn't want to go to lunch with us?"

"She totally did." His daughter gave him a pitying look. "Women can tell these things."

"You're not a woman. You're a menace." He frowned. "What if she's a vegetarian?"

"Daddy." Madison shook her head and walked up to the counter. She smiled at the woman behind the counter. "We're buying those books, and I'd like a hot chocolate, please. And a Madeleine."

"Sure thing, honey." The woman winked at him as she picked up a carton of milk. "You big into romance, sugar, or are you into Lola?"

"Both," his daughter answered for him.

"Two life sentences," he promised her as he slid the books across the counter. "And you have to clean the bathroom."

Madison giggled and hugged him around his waist.

Touchdown Taylor, buying romance novels. He could hear the guys in the locker room giving him a hard time.

Then he saw the back cover of the book, with Lola's beautiful face smiling on it, and he was surprised by the urge to pick it up to read. Not that he'd tell anyone that—not the boys, not his daughter, and especially not Ms. Lola Carmichael.

Somehow Lola found herself sitting in a booth at a burger joint in the outer Richmond, having burgers and fries with Sam Taylor and his daughter. She could hardly believe it, and she was sitting there, living it.

Sam and Madison shared the other side of the booth. Sam had his arm draped over the seatback and he casually played with the end of Madison's ponytail. Madison leaned toward him as she ate and talked about her friends at school.

Chewing thoughtfully, she listened to them banter. They had a good relationship—that much was obvious. Sam doted on Madison, and Madison clearly worshipped her father, even if she gave him a hard time.

Astonishing. Lola took another fry as she watched their interaction. She missed her dad. They hadn't had quite the same easy camaraderie that Sam and Madison had, but she'd never doubted that he'd loved her.

Madison turned to her. "What do you think, Lola?"

She shook her head. "I was daydreaming. What do I think about what?"

"Bras."

She looked at Sam. By the furrow of his brow, she took it that he didn't like this conversation. So she said, "I have a friend who sells bras. Well, really all lingerie, but especially bras. She thinks they're very important."

"Really?" Madison perked up. "Can I go to her store? I think it's time to get one."

Lola glanced quickly at the girl's still-adolescent chest. "What do your parents think?"

"Mom's busy with her social life, and Daddy says I can't have one until I'm thirty."

Glancing at Sam, Lola tried not to smile. "I'm sure your daddy knows what's best for you."

Madison whirled to her dad. "Sarah Michelle says I'll get *saggy* if I don't start wearing a bra now."

The girl didn't have enough to even threaten drooping, but Lola could see Sam didn't want to point that out, so she said, "I didn't wear a bra until I was fifteen, and I don't sag."

"Really?" Madison gaze went directly to Lola's boobs. "They do look nice."

Sam cleared his throat. "Can we change the topic?"

"Would you rather we talk about jock straps, Daddy?"

"Hell, no." He frowned at his daughter. "You better not know anything about them either."

The girl tossed her napkin aside. "Let's go to a movie."

"I promised your mom I'd have you home early to finish your homework."

"I'd rather watch a movie with you guys." She looked at the two of them eagerly. "Unless you'd rather go alone so you could make out."

Lola's gaze shot to Sam's. She could tell he was remembering their kiss in the sound room. She felt herself flush at the hungry way he looked at her now.

He was the one to recover first, saying, "Madison, you *especially* better not know what making out is."

"We have cable, Daddy. It's not like I live in a hole."

"Careful, or I'll see that you do." He looked at Lola. "I'll take this little monster home first and then drop you off."

She covered up the odd surge of disappointment with a bright smile. "Sounds great."

Madison sat in the back even though Lola tried to get her to take the front seat. The Jeep was big, but Sam was huge. He seemed to energetically spill into her space.

Sitting so close to Sam was...

Nerve-wracking.

Awful.

Exhilarating.

She ran through a thesaurus of words in her head to keep herself from reaching over to take his hand.

He pulled over to the curb and put the car in park. Turning to her, he said, "Excuse me a sec."

"Bye, Lola." Madison threw her arms around Lola's neck, strangling her enthusiastically from behind. "I can't wait to read your book, even if Daddy won't let me for five years."

"Ten," he threatened, winking at Lola. He opened the door and escorted his bouncy daughter to her mother's home.

Lola exhaled deeply the second they were gone. She tried to regroup, but it was hard. All her preconceived notions about Sam *Touchdown* Taylor were being proven wrong. In fact, Sam was charming her with the obvious way he loved his daughter.

Sam came back a moment later. As he got in and buckled up, he said, "I half expected you to have run home after all that."

She smiled. "Madison is something."

"That's an understatement." He turned to her and grinned like a father besotted by his child. "She's pretty terrific, isn't she?"

Lola's heart melted, and in that moment she decided she liked him. A lot.

"Where do you live?" he asked, pulling away from the curb.

"Back by Grounds for Thoughts, in Laurel Heights. On Sacramento."

"Fancy."

She shrugged. "Convenient."

She felt him looking at her, wanting to know more. But she wasn't about to confess that she'd moved there to be close to her mother. She didn't want to explain how her mom had been slowly disappearing over the past ten years, her memories slipping away, bit by bit. That, after years of experimental drugs and trying to take care of her mom herself, Lola had finally had to put her in a special home.

Looking out the window, she turned the conver-

sation back onto him. "How long have you been divorced?"

"Not long enough. Three years." He was quiet for a moment and then said, "Chelsea became pregnant *accidentally* after I was offered a running back position on the 49ers. But I blew out my knee soon after, and she wasn't happy about being a has-been's wife. I stuck in there for Madison's sake, though."

"I can't believe I read you so wrong."

"How so?" he asked, glancing at her.

"I thought you were a total bastard."

"I am."

"You're actually a nice guy." She shook her head. "I know. I'm surprised by that, too."

They drove in silence until they reached her building. He double-parked outside and walked her up to her apartment.

She was conscious of him behind her every step of the way. He watched her butt—she could feel it. And because she could feel it, she may have added just a touch more attitude to its sway as she walked.

At her door, she unlocked it and turned around. Before she could thank him, he pressed her against it and kissed her.

She gave herself up to him instantly, arching up to meet him, wrapping her arms around his neck. She felt one of his hands cradle her head and the other anchor her by the waist.

Just like the last time, the kiss consumed her. The passion, the heat—she'd never felt anything like it.

The first time hadn't been a fluke.

"This is crazy," he murmured against her mouth as he slipped his hand under the layers of her clothing to the bare skin of her back.

She sighed in pleasure and nodded. "Totally crazy."

"I don't seem to mind that much though." He clasped her close and rewarded her with another enthusiastic onslaught.

She hitched her leg over his hip, rubbing against the very prominent ridge of his erection. Frankly, she didn't mind either. At all.

"I have an idea," he said after kissing her so boneless she could have qualified for whatever genus earthworms belonged to.

She nodded and said, "Yes," before she kissed him more.

When he came up for air, he pointed out, "You

don't even know what I'm going to suggest."

"No, but I'm sure it's an excellent idea." She lifted her lips for more.

But he just smiled down at her. "I was going to suggest me bringing over dinner tomorrow. After my show."

"Okay." She rubbed herself against him, focusing on the now.

"Okay. Good." He nodded and then disentangled from her.

Lola blinked in surprise. "What are you doing?"

"Going home to give us a chance to cool down and reconsider the biggest mistake we've both made in a long time."

She frowned. "How does that make sense?"

"It doesn't." He shook his head. "In fact, in half an hour I'm going to beat my head against the wall for passing up a chance to 'make out' with the hottest woman I've ever met."

Lola perked up. "Really?"

"You know you are." He laid another wickedly intense kiss on her before he turned and jogged down the stairs. "Think about it, Lola. Tomorrow night."

His sexy voice promised a night of unimaginable

delights—and she had an *excellent* imagination. She slumped against the door, fanning herself. There was nothing to think about. She was going to be ready for him tomorrow night.

Chapter Nine

THE BENEFITS OF having a boss like Eve was that when you wanted to leave work early to stalk a man, she just said "Good luck."

Kristin settled on the step in front of the locked lobby to the apartments above Grounds for Thought. She had no idea where Rob Cray lived, but she knew he walked by the café every day on the way to and from work.

This past week, he'd taken the puppy with him.

She'd been so surprised when she saw him walk into the café that first morning with the dog trotting obediently next to him on a brand-new leash. She hadn't been entirely sure that he'd keep the bedraggled thing, but the fact that he had reinforced her decision to ask him to father her child. He had compassion, and she liked that.

"Excuse me."

Kristin looked up at the gravelly voice. In front of her stood a hulk of a man: tall, muscles bulging from a tight T-shirt, longish Johnny Depp hair. His gaze was so intense that if she hadn't been sitting she'd have backed up a couple steps.

She swallowed. "Yes?"

"You're in my way." He nodded at the door.

"You live here?" Then it registered on her who he was. "*Oh*. You're the new guy who rented Eve's apartment."

He simply stared at her.

It'd have scared a normal person, but Kristin had been raised with two older brothers. She could tell he was all bark. "They say you're a serial killer."

He continued to stare at her.

"So you're not wanted in five states?"

"Move," he said.

She stood up, not getting out of his way entirely. "Ogres usually live under bridges, not in San Francisco flats."

He stepped up, towering over her. "Do you have a death wish?"

Shrugging, she said, "I need a little excitement in my life."

He stared at her, a blank look that betrayed nothing. Then he brushed by her and let himself into the building.

"Are you okay?"

She turned to find Rob and the puppy a few feet away. Chanel was straining at her leash, growling after the intense dude. Rob wasn't much better.

"I'm great. Don't worry about him. He got jock itch at the gym and it's pissing him off." Kristin gestured behind her. "We're besties, actually."

Rob's frown deepened.

She bent down to pet the dog, who had a sparkly collar around its neck that read Chanel. It was silly, but Kristin felt tingly that Rob had not only kept the name she'd given the dog but given her a personalized collar with it, too.

She smiled brilliantly, scratching the dog behind her ears. "How are you doing, Chanel? It looks like you've been to the spa."

"I've never seen a dog like the groomer the way this one did," Rob said. "She didn't want to leave."

"I like the spa too," she told the animal. Then she stood. "Of course, I haven't been in forever. Is that takeout in your hand?"

He looked down at the bag he was carrying. "Yes."

She waited for him to elaborate, but when he didn't she asked, "What kind?"

"Indian."

"I love Indian food." She beamed at him. "Mind if I join you?"

The puppy barked once.

"Chanel thinks it's a good idea," she pointed out with a sweet smile.

"What's your game?" he asked suspiciously.

She froze, hearing her slowly desiccating eggs scream to tread carefully. "What do you mean?"

"You obviously want something from me."

Your sperm, but she didn't think he'd react well if she told him that now. So she just said, "I like you."

His jaw steeled. "I'm not an easy mark, so if you're after money you picked the wrong guy."

The idea that she'd want money was so ludicrous that she burst out laughing. Then she thought about it more and doubled over.

"It's not that funny," she heard Rob say over her laughter.

If he knew what was in her bank account—the one in the states as well as the one she'd opened in the

Grand Caymans, just because it tickled her—he'd laugh too.

Or maybe not. Men were touchy about their women out-earning them. Unless they were mooches, and she took care not to attract the sort of man who'd try to take advantage of her.

"Want to clue me in on the joke?" Rob asked, with curiosity rather than the annoyance she'd have expected.

Wiping the tears of mirth, she shook her head. "Not today. Or at least not until you feed me."

He sighed. "Come on."

She walked alongside him, hiccupping the occasional last bit of laughter. "I haven't had that good a laugh in a while."

"I'm glad I could help."

"Just to clarify, I was laughing at me, not you."

"If you want me to believe that, you'll have to deliver it more convincingly."

She grinned. "I'm an awful actress. I'm pretty much an open book. I never learned feminine wiles because I was surrounded by boys. My mom was no help, because she was a firefighter."

"Your mom?"

She nodded. "We were a rough and tumble household. I'm scrappy. Don't ever try to arm wrestle me. I don't play fair."

"I could have told you that," he muttered.

Chanel barked in agreement.

"I love this dog." She smiled at the pooch. "I'm so happy you decided to adopt her."

"She's not so bad." He bent down and scratched its ears.

Aw. Robert Cray pretended like he was a cold-ass business guy but he was mush on the inside.

Then Kristin frowned. "What *do* you do for a living, Rob?"

"I run a hedge fund."

Successfully, based on the way he dressed and that he lived in Laurel Heights.

They walked down the block and turned right. Another block, a left turn, and he nodded at a house. "It's this one."

She stood outside and looked at the building. It was a three-story Edwardian cottage, nicely maintained with a small but lovely front yard. "It's so cute," she exclaimed as she hurried to follow him to the porch.

He opened the door and motioned her inside.

She strode in and looked around. "It's a whole house."

"Yes." He looked at her like she was insane. Bending, he unlatched Chanel's leash.

The dog calmly trotted down the hallway, obviously knowing where she was going.

Kristin ducked into the first doorway. There was a large living room, decorated in shades of brown. Expensively decorated, but monochromatic nonetheless. "How many bedrooms do you have?"

"Four." He pulled off his tie, setting it neatly on a table, and unbuttoned the top couple buttons of his shirt.

She gawked at his neck. For some reason, that small patch of skin was more erotic than anything she'd ever seen.

She was in a worse way than she realized. Clearing her throat, she averted her gaze to avoid jumping him. "And you live alone? With all this space?"

"No. Thanks to you, I live with Chanel." The corner of his mouth hitched in a smile. "At least she prefers sleeping in her own bed. I figured her for a bed hog. This way."

She followed him down the hall, unabashedly sticking her nose into every room they passed. She could tell it was professionally decorated because everything was perfect. But it was a house, not a home—a little cold and not lived in. "Your house is big. Do you want a family?"

"I haven't thought about it specifically, but it's in my long-term plans."

"Good."

He glanced at her over his shoulder.

"It'd be a shame to waste all this space," she said blithely. He didn't need to hear the thoughts formulating in her head.

"I usually eat in the study." He handed her the food and gestured her into a room. "Make yourself comfortable. I'll be back with silverware."

"Okay." She walked in, set the bag of food down, and began to snoop.

This room was infinitely homier than the rest of the house. It wasn't as sterile or perfect, but still had the neatness she realized was part of who Rob was. There were personal touches in here. A photo of an older couple on his desk. Some more obviously family photos on a wall. Some well-worn books on a shelf.

A cashmere throw casually tossed on the back of a leather couch.

This was where he lived. She bet his bedroom was similarly tidy but lived in.

He walked in and put the tray he carried on the coffee table. "Did you find what you were looking for?" he asked wryly as he sat on the couch.

Not yet, but she was closer to unlocking him. She held up the frame from his desk. "Are these your parents?"

"Yes."

She looked at them. She could see a resemblance to both of them, along with the aloofness she'd come to expect from him. He came by it naturally. At least it wasn't her, she thought as she set the photo down. Instead of sitting on the couch, she sat on the floor next to him because it seemed less formal. "Do they live in San Francisco?"

"Boston."

"Do you visit them often? Do they visit you? Are you close to them? And are the people in the other pictures your brothers and sisters?"

He gave her an amused look as he took out the containers of food from the bag. "I'm not sure where to start with that barrage of questions, so how about if I ask you some?"

She blinked. "Why?"

"Why are you asking me questions?"

"Because you interest me. We've already established that I'm just a pest you're feeding."

He stopped in mid-motion and stared at her.

She tried to figure out what he saw. She knew she was attractive enough, but looks didn't matter. What mattered was the connection between the two of them—the electricity that flashed whenever they were close.

Did he recognize that?

"I tend to exterminate pests," he said carefully.

"Is that a warning?"

He chuckled and handed her a plate. "That's a statement of fact that has nothing to do with you, as you're not a pest. Much."

"Thanks." She grinned. "When do we get married?"

He did a double take but relaxed when he saw she was obviously joking. "What I'm trying to figure out is what you want from me," he said, handing her a container of curry.

"I want your body," she said, scooping a generous

portion onto her plate before handing it back to him.

"You do," he agreed, giving her a foil packet of *naan*. "But that's not going to happen."

"Why not?" She set the bread down, engrossed in the conversation.

"It wouldn't work out."

"How do you know?" she insisted.

"I just do."

"Yet you still invited me over."

He shook his head. "You invited yourself."

"You could have said no."

"To you, apparently I can't."

To her, that meant she was irresistible, which was a good thing. But he obviously felt differently about it. "You don't look happy about that."

"I told you, I can't figure it out. You should be an annoyance but..."

"But what?" she asked.

She didn't think he'd answer, but finally he said, "But I'm intrigued, even though I shouldn't be."

"Why shouldn't you be intrigued? Because I'm unacceptable?" A thought occurred to her. "Is this because I work in a café and you have a 'real'"—she made air quotes—"job?"

"Not entirely."

"You know that means yes." Frowning, she tore a piece of *naan* and dipped it into the curry on her plate. "For the record, I love working at Grounds for Thought, much more than I liked what I did before. I get to talk to an assortment of people, and they all look forward to coming in and spending time with me."

"What did you do before?"

"Tech stuff." He didn't need to know she'd built one of the world's most successful technology consulting firms.

"And now you're a barista." He said it like he was trying to understand it. "Why did you stop working in tech? Were you laid off?"

"It was time to move on." She saw he translated that as *Yes, I got laid off,* but she didn't do anything to correct his impression. She pushed her food away, no longer hungry. "Light the fire for me."

He frowned. "It's not cold out."

"Where's the romance in you?" She rolled her eyes. "Who cares? It'll be nice."

He looked like he wanted to tell her there was no romance between them, but he surprised her by

lighting it. It was one of those automatic gas fireplaces, and the heat radiated from it immediately.

Sighing, she crawled closer and stretched out her legs, rolling her feet. She wasn't used to standing on her feet all day. "Eve, my boss, works in these crazy high heels. I have no idea how she does it."

Rob glanced at her feet. She could see him contemplate massaging her feet. He didn't, but that was okay with her because he considered it. Baby steps.

"Are you done eating?" he asked.

"Yes. Thank you."

"You barely had anything."

"You ruined my appetite."

"Because I said we'd never have a relationship?"

"Yes." She turned to face him. "Correct me if I'm wrong, but I assumed you were there when we kissed last time."

His gaze fell to her lips. "I was there."

She heard the desire in his voice and threw her hands up. "Then why are you determined not to get involved with me? We nearly went up in flames, and all we did was touch lips. Just think if we did more."

"No, I will not think about that."

"Why the heck not?" She growled in frustration.

"You just said you were interested."

"I shouldn't be. We're in different places in our lives. You need to be thinking about your career options at your age."

"What age?"

"You're, what, in your mid-to-late twenties?"

She laughed while her thirty-eight year old eggs wailed in despair. "I wonder if that's a compliment or if you're telling me I'm immature."

"How old are you?" he asked, obviously confused.

"Old enough to know I want you." She slinked over to him.

"What are you doing?" he asked, though he remained completely still and watchful.

She may be doing the preying, but she had the sense he was still the predator there. She crawled onto his lap, straddling him. "I'm going to kiss you."

His hands held her by her hips, neither encouraging nor discouraging. "That's not a good idea."

"It's the best idea I've acted on in a long time." She tilted her head and brought her mouth to his. The first kiss was glancing, testing, but still warm.

The second kiss held none of the initial hesitation. She dove in, going for it. His hands stayed where

they were, but they tightened on her.

She lifted her head just enough to whisper against his lips, "Is this onerous for you?"

"No."

"Then kiss me back." She shifted closer. "Like you mean it."

He gazed into her eyes as if searching for her motives. But, frankly, whatever motive she had before, right then she only wanted him for himself.

He snaked his hand into her hair, tipped her head back, and kissed her deep. It was slow and thorough, but as instantly hot as the fireplace. All her various body parts came alive.

Throwing her arms around him, she pressed her body to his. Under his dress shirt, he felt solid. Manly. Her girlie parts sighed in pleasure and anticipation.

Her soul sighed. *Him,* it insisted.

She had to agree.

It was just starting to get interesting when Rob lifted his mouth and said, "I'll take you home now."

She just wanted him to take her—period. But she didn't want to push him when she'd won this skirmish. So she sat back. "I'll get home on my own."

"I'm taking you."

"I live across town. It doesn't make sense for you to go all the way there and back." Plus she didn't want him to see her posh flat.

He set her on the couch next to him. "I'm taking you. Let's go."

She huffed, but she knew she wasn't going to win here.

In the car, he said, "Where am I going?"

"Potrero Hill."

He arched a brow as he navigated through the empty San Francisco streets. "A little upscale."

"Not my place." Not compared to his. "I've been there a while, and I share it."

It wasn't even that much of a lie. She did share the building with another couple, but the top floor and its views of the city were all hers.

They drove in silence, both obviously wrapped in their own thoughts. When they pulled up to her place, she pointed to the side gate. "I'm that way."

"You live in the back?" he asked, looking out the window.

"Yeah." That wasn't much of a lie either. Her bedroom was in the back, and she *did* spend most of her time there.

She opened the door. "Thank you for feeding me."

"You didn't eat."

"And for bringing me home."

"Grudgingly."

"Are you always this difficult, or is this for my benefit?" she asked, exasperated.

He had the nerve to grin. "It's mostly you."

Eyes narrowed, she grabbed his shirt and kissed him. She meant it to be punishing, but it was charged and left her yearning for more.

Before he could tell her to stop, she ran out of the car and up the walkway to the gate. She let herself in and watched him from behind it, waiting for him to leave before going in, turning on all the lights, and dropping onto her bed.

She'd meant to ask him to be her sperm donor, but now she was confused. She propped a pillow under her head and stared sightlessly at the ceiling. Now she wondered if she wasn't shortchanging herself and her baby by just asking him to be a donor. Because she could see herself sitting on the floor with him, eating Indian food and bantering, for years to come.

Maybe her plans needed to be adjusted. Maybe she hadn't been thinking big enough.

Sighing, she relived every delicious kiss from the night and imagined having that forever.

Chapter Ten

LOLA'S FRONT DOOR buzzed at 10:10pm, exactly ten minutes after Sam had said his show would end. The nerves in her belly that had been jittery all day flared into full flight as she went to let him in.

She opened the door. "Hi—"

He dropped the bag in his hand, pulled her to him, and devoured her.

The moment his lips touched hers, her nerves were forgotten. She wrapped her arms around his waist, burrowing under his jacket as his hands speared into her hair. She heard him groan as his hand touched the skin under her robe and he realized she wasn't wearing anything under it.

His mouth took hers as passionately as every time before. Hungrier this time. Deeper, and a bit slower, as if they both knew they had all night.

He walked her backwards without breaking

their kiss. She heard the door shut behind them, and he blindly reached behind to lock the deadbolt. Then he hauled her up, hands under her butt, and turned her to the nearest wall.

She gasped in excitement and anchored her legs around him. His hard-on, which seemed ever-ready, jutted against her. She rubbed herself on it, hoping she conveyed just how eager she was for this.

Sam trailed kisses on her neck as he untied her robe. "Please tell me you've been naked waiting like this for me all day."

"Does that make you hot?" She pulled his T-shirt out of his jeans to get to the skin underneath.

"It'll keep me hot for the next month." He pushed the robe off one shoulder and bit her skin lightly.

"In that case, I write like this all day." She arched her back, offering him more. "Naked, in a silky robe, just me and my laptop."

Groaning again, he pressed against her so she felt the pulse of his hardness. "You know I'm going to think about that all the time, right?"

"Good." She reclaimed his mouth.

He undid his pants, and when she felt his hot flesh against her thigh it was her turn to moan.

"I need help with this," he said, holding up a condom.

That she could do. She tore it open and sheathed him as quickly as humanly possible with her pressed against the wall and him nibbling on her. Not wanting to leave anything for chance, she guided him into her.

They both gasped at the feeling.

"It feels"—she struggled to find the words—"full."

"And warm." He kept himself hovering at her entrance, letting her get used to the feel of him. Brushing her hair out of her face, he held her gaze. "You still good with this?"

"No." She wiggled on him. "I'm excellent with this."

"Thank God," he said fervently, and then he thrust all the way into her.

Her head fell back automatically, and she thumped it hard against the wall. "Ow."

"I'll kiss it better," Sam promised her, "after I kiss this."

And he latched onto her nipple and sucked.

She cried out, her legs tightening around him of their own volition. By the way that he groaned, she could tell he liked that, so she squeezed harder.

He thrust into her, going faster and faster until she had to grab onto his shoulders, kneading her fingers in and holding on.

It was the best ride of her life.

It was the kind of sex the characters in her books had.

At least usually—she couldn't seem to get Louise and Calvin to get it on.

"What are you thinking about?" Sam said, his breathing labored.

"Isn't that the girl's line?"

"Not when you're suddenly not paying attention to what's going on here." He shifted back, just enough to work his hand between their bodies. "Maybe this will help," he said as he touched her there.

She cried out, her fingers and toes curling.

"Do I have your attention again?" he whispered against her neck.

"Yes." She rolled her hips. He touched her infuriatingly lightly, and she needed more.

As if he read her mind, he asked, "More?"

"Yes." She pushed against him. "Yes, yes, *yes*."

He gave her what she wanted, everything she

asked for. His finger pressed her harder, until her vision clouded and every slide of his erection into her was a cascade of fireworks.

"That's it, sweetheart," he murmured. "Work me. Come on me, for me."

She cried out, unable to stop herself from falling into climax. It rolled over her, through her—over and over. She vaguely registered him calling out her name as he followed her, his fingers digging into her flesh.

Unable to hold herself up, she slumped against him. Holding her, he let them slide carefully down the wall until he held her on his lap, a heap in his arms.

She closed her eyes, listening to his heartbeat. Strong and rapid, it seemed to echo hers.

Seemed was the operative word there. This was a hook up. A casual thing, she reminded herself. A carnal impulse that neither one of them could deny.

Whatever. It was good. "Are we going to do that again?" she asked drowsily.

"Yes." He rolled onto his back, pulling her on top of him.

"I didn't mean now." She managed to lift her head to look at him. "Unless you can just do it on command."

He pressed deeper inside her. "Want to give it a try?"

She felt him grow harder in her and sighed in pleasure. "Yes, please. And then I'll need to eat."

"I'll need to eat too," he whispered with a wicked grin before feasting—on her.

Using chopsticks, Lola popped a piece of broccoli into her mouth. She loved Chinese food, but it was infinitely more delicious while sitting naked in bed.

Of course, it had at least a little to do with the long, hunky man sprawled sideways across the mattress. He was propped on his arm, watching her as he slowly ate an egg roll.

She grinned. The sheets had been shoved off the end of the bed and her hair felt like it had a Medusa thing going on, but she couldn't remember feeling this good in a long time.

Sam's fault, but she bet he was more than willing to take the blame.

She pointed the chopsticks at his flaccid yet still impressive manly parts. "You must have been hated in the locker room."

He looked down at himself. "Is that some strange romance writer way of saying you like the package?"

"It's quite a package." She looked down at his scarred knee.

He sighed. "We were in Tahoe, and I got angry with Chelsea, my ex, so I decided to work out my frustration on the slopes. My career ended with one unlucky run. It was the second most stupid thing I've ever done."

"The first?"

"Marrying Chelsea." He smiled self-deprecatingly.

"But you have Madison now," Lola pointed out.

"Yes. And I have my radio show." He frowned. "Or I will again, after I finish with *Ladies' Night*."

"That seems like a strange career move."

"They thought I'd pumped the ratings." He dipped egg roll in the pink sauce and offered her a bite.

It was sweet and greasy and delicious. "You got here really quickly from the station."

"I ran a couple stop signs." He grinned sheepishly. "I also had an intern pick up the food for me. I didn't want to waste time getting here."

"I like that you were eager."

"I like that you greeted me naked."

"I didn't greet you naked. I had a robe on."

He wrapped his hand around her ankle. "Wear that robe for me more often."

Lola glowed in womanly satisfaction. "Okay."

Taking the box out of her hand, Sam deftly grabbed some beef with his chopsticks. "About us."

She stilled. "Us?"

"I want to make sure we're on the same page."

"What page is that?" she asked carefully.

"The page that repeats as often as we like, without strings."

"Oh." Relieved, she nodded. "That sounds great."

"It does?" he asked, also being careful.

"Yes." She picked up the last egg roll. "I'm not about to get invested in another emotionally bankrupt man, and no playboy is going to want to settle down."

"Just to be clear, I'm the playboy in this scenario?"

"Duh." She winked at him and offered him a bit of the soggy egg roll.

"Is that what you want?" he asked after he'd chewed. "To settle down?"

"All women want a Happily Ever After."

"Some women want money."

Something in his voice caught her attention. She looked at him—really looked at him. He tried to appear casual but he was bothered. She remembered what he'd said about his ex-wife and her heart broke for him. "Not all women," she assured him softly. "Some women just want someone who'll see their flaws and love them anyway."

"What are your flaws?"

"I write." She shrugged. "Sometimes a lot. Sometimes in the evenings or late at night. Some guys can't handle not being the center of a woman's world."

He shrugged. "Some guys appreciate a woman who's independent."

"I also have other family obligations." She thought of her mother and had to shore up her smile.

"So do I."

Knowing he was talking about his daughter, she said, "I love Madison."

"She's a terror, but she's mine."

"You love her, too."

"In a deep and abiding way I never knew existed," he said, unabashed.

Longing pierced her chest. "That's so sweet. She's

a lucky girl."

"You didn't have that sort of relationship with your father?"

"My dad died when I was twenty." She smiled as thought about how hard he'd tried to treat her like an adult instead of his baby. "He was a good father. Our relationship was just starting to mature into something special when he passed away."

"You must have been devastated when he died."

"My mom was more devastated than anyone." She swallowed thickly. Sally's grief had been thick and heavy, and Lola hadn't been able to do anything to help. Sometimes she wondered if it hadn't brought on the dementia. Sometimes she wondered if it wasn't a blessing that her mom couldn't remember what she'd lost. "They were the most in-love couple I'd ever seen. When he died, Mom was lost."

"Is your mom okay now?"

Her mom would never be okay, but it felt too personal a thing to talk about. So she put on her shored-up smile. "Mom is great."

He fed her a bite of beef. "I feel sad for your dad."

"Why?"

"He didn't get to see how lovely you turned out."

Tears prickled her eyes. From anyone else and she'd have doubted their sincerity, but Sam meant it—she could tell. She blinked away the moisture, feeling her heart soften against him.

Bad, *bad* idea. He might not be the cretin she originally thought, but that didn't mean anything. Kevin hadn't been a jerk at first either. She didn't have the emotional reserves to take that chance. Not when she had a book—a bestseller—due and a sick mother to take care of.

So she pushed aside all the food and brought them back to level ground by pouring herself over him.

"Hello," he said huskily, his arms going around her. "Enough food?"

She nodded as she straddled his hips. "I'm ready for dessert."

Chapter Eleven

GROUNDS FOR THOUGHT was slammed.

It happened sometimes. Kristin was used to working in tandem with Eve behind the counter. She looked at it like an intricate choreography, sometimes graceful, sometimes clumsy.

It was so different than when she worked at Aspire. At Aspire, if she wanted to, she could work for days without talking with anyone face-to-face.

Despite the morning craziness, Kristin was aware that Rob hadn't come in at his normal time. Every time someone came in, she glanced at the door, hopeful it'd be him.

Silly, she chided herself as she handed a customer an iced coffee. It was past nine—he was long at work already.

Had she turned him off that night she'd invited herself to his place for dinner?

Frowning, she slowly steamed milk for a mocha and cappuccino. She replayed the evening in her head. She *had* been a little pushy, but he hadn't seemed turned off.

Neither had he been chomping at the bit to get involved with her. And she hadn't seen him at the café since.

She pouted as she finished the drinks and slid them across the counter.

"A vanilla latte, a Nutella latte, and a double espresso for here," her boss said, as she handed change to a customer. "And I need a smile from my barista."

Kristin sighed. "Am I that bad?"

"Yes." Eve smiled at her. "But it's just withdrawal because your guy hasn't been in yet."

"It's way late. He's not—"

The other woman nudged her. "Look."

He walked in, eyes on her.

Oh, please, him, her body sighed. She went through the usual barrage of feelings: the tingles, the shivers, and the hot flashes.

Frankly, it was like the flu.

"If you glare at him like that, you'll scare the poor

guy," Eve said as she leaned to bag a scone.

"I'm not glaring at him," she protested, pouring a cup of coffee. "I'm conveying my displeasure over his lack of apparent interest."

"He doesn't look disinterested." Her boss openly appraised him. "He looks like he wants to lick whipped cream off every inch of your body."

Kristin snorted and tried to ignore him.

It was impossible. He drew her eyes. It was more than his looks—it was *him*. She found him irresistible in a way she'd never experienced. It was disconcerting and exciting all at once. It didn't help that he really was watching her like he wanted her, just like Eve said. His stare was like a caress, and she felt it all over her body.

She was conscious of him the whole while, even though she ducked her head and hid behind the huge espresso machine. He placed his order with her boss and then stood across from her waiting for his coffee.

Kristin pointed a stirrer at him. "I don't have time to flirt today, so don't even try it."

"There's always time for flirting," Eve said, taking the silver spoon from her. "Take it in the kitchen."

She gestured to the line. "There's a ton of people."

"I'll handle it until Allison arrives." Eve checked the time. "She'll be here in minutes. Go."

Kristin frowned at Rob. "He doesn't want to."

"I don't recall being asked," he replied mildly.

"Fine. Gang up on me." She threw her hands in the air. Walking out from behind the counter, she grabbed Rob by the tie. "Come on."

He gently untangled the silk from her hand as they walked, holding her hand instead.

"Don't think that's going to mollify me," she tossed over her shoulder as they walked into the kitchen.

He tugged her to a stop and turned her to face him. "Want to tell me what's got you worked up?"

"I'm not worked up." She crossed her arms. "I'm peeved."

Humor lit his eyes.

She punched his shoulder. "Don't you dare laugh."

"I wouldn't even think of it."

"That's the problem, isn't it? You wouldn't think of it." She huffed. "Well, I'm done, then."

"Why do women always expect you to read their minds?" He shook his head. "I have no idea what you're talking about. What didn't I think of?"

"Me." She crossed her arms and glared at him. "Sex with me, to be exact."

"That's ridiculous. I think of that all the time."

She started to yell at him, and then his words registered. "You do?"

"How could I not, when you throw your incredible body at me and kiss me like you do?" He shook his head, eyebrows drawn.

"You don't look especially pleased about it," she accused.

"I'm not." He stalked toward her. "You harass me. You stalk me. You acquired me a dog I didn't want—"

"Don't talk about Chanel that way. She's sensitive."

"—And you disrupt my mornings with your sassy mouth, so that all I can think of for the first hour at work is kissing you. You're driving me crazy."

She backed up slowly. "I don't mean to drive you crazy."

"Yes, you do." He trapped her against a counter, his arms bracketing either side of her. "You're trying to get me to lose control."

Heart pounding, she looked up at him. "Am I succeeding?"

"I never lose control," he said as he cupped the back of her head and pressed closer.

Then he kissed her.

She mewled in pleasure the moment his lips touched hers. It was deliberate and in charge so all she could do was wrap her arms around him and hold on.

When he finally let her go, she propped her hands on the counter so she wouldn't ooze to the ground. "That was nice," she said. "We'll have to try it again."

"No."

"No?" She wrinkled her nose.

"No." He straightened his tie.

She waited for more, but it became apparent he wasn't going to say more, so she said, "Why not? Didn't you just say you think of me like I think of you?"

"Yes, but that doesn't mean getting involved with each other is a good idea."

She wanted to say she didn't want to get involved, that she just wanted to have sex, but it felt like a lie. So she just said, "It's a great idea."

He smoothed her hair back in place. "We'd be a train wreck."

"We'd be fireworks."

"More like the explosion from two trains colliding." He caressed her face. "We live in different worlds. It wouldn't work. I've tried it before."

They weren't from different worlds, but it seemed important for him to accept her as she was, not because he found out she had a gazillion dollars and used to head one of the largest tech firms in the world. "Lady and the Tramp made it work."

The corner of his lips quirked. "You're using Disney as an example for us?"

"It works." She looked behind him. "Speaking of Lady, where's Chanel?"

"At the vet, getting her check up. That's why I'm late to work." He glanced at his watch. "I had to wait to drop her off."

Her heart melted. He'd be such a good dad.

"I have to get to work," he said.

She grasped his tie before he could get away. "Where you'll think about me and my sassy mouth?"

His gaze fell to said mouth. "I won't think about you, Kristin."

She gave him a gentle kiss and whispered against his lips. "Liar."

Chapter Twelve

SAM HUDDLED ON the living room couch, feeling like he was a kid hiding from his parents. Except in reality, he was the parent and the person he was hiding from was his daughter.

The text came through in an optimistic ping.

LOLA CARMICHAEL: *I got the flowers today.*

He'd never sent flowers to a woman after he'd spent the night—or rather, two nights. It wasn't his style, but he'd been passing the flower stand and they looked like her, bright and sunny. So he'd acted on impulse.

Before he could reply, she texted him again.

LOLA CARMICHAEL: *You don't need to butter me up to get into my pants again. Make me come like that again and you can come over anytime.*

"I'll be right over," he murmured as he pecked at his phone.

SAM TAYLOR: *That assumes you're wearing pants.*

LOLA CARMICHAEL: *You wish, big boy.*

"Whatchya doing, Daddy?"

Like he was going to tell her. "Did you finish your homework?"

She rolled her eyes as she bounced down next to him. "A way long time ago. I told you."

"Oh. Right." He'd been distracted. Actually, he'd been distracted constantly since he'd left Lola Sunday morning. The two nights with her had shifted the axis of his world.

"Who were you texting?" His daughter tried to dodge around him to look at his screen.

"No one." He turned off his screen. The last thing he needed was for his daughter to see him sexting a woman.

Madison made a face at him and then grabbed the remote. She turned the TV off.

"Hey." He pointed at the blank screen. "That's Monday Night Football."

"We have important things to discuss, and I want you to pay attention," she said in her attempt of a grown up voice. "If the TV's on you won't listen."

Important things? He imagined all the things it could be—all the female related things—and started to sweat. "Maybe we should call your Mom."

Madison's face wrinkled adorably. "To talk about Lola?"

"Lola?" He frowned. "This is about Lola?"

"What did you think it was about? *Sex*?" she shrieked in a purposeful taunt.

He pointed at her. "It's not nice to tease your father."

She giggled.

"So what do you want to talk about?"

"I think you should take her to your party thing on Friday."

"I told you about that?"

"Duh." She rolled her eyes. "Ask her."

He pictured Lola in a cocktail dress and he started to sweat again. "Madison, I don't think she'll want to go."

"Sure she will. All girls like a reason to wear fancy dresses. And she likes you."

"How do you know?"

She shrugged with eleven-year-old wisdom. "It's totally obvious. So are you going to ask her?"

"I'll think about it." Actually, it was brilliant. Jennifer was going to be there, of course, since it was a station-sponsored fundraiser. If she thought that he and Lola cared about each other, maybe she'd put him back into his normal spot.

Truthfully, *Ladies' Night* wasn't as bad as he thought it'd be. Once he got over his initial negative headspace, he'd been surprised to realize he enjoyed the program. People cared about his opinions on their love lives, and his guest were entertaining.

Not that he wanted to be stuck dishing out advice to lovesick women for the rest of his life. He loved sports.

And Lola was the answer to the situation with Jennifer.

However, he had a feeling Lola wouldn't like it if she knew what he was considering doing.

But she wouldn't have to know, and he actually did like her. It surprised him. He felt awake with her in a way he hadn't been since he'd played football. So, technically, this was win-win.

"Don't think about it." Madison grabbed his phone and shoved it in his face. "Do it."

He scowled at her but took the phone from her

hand. "When did you get so pushy?"

"You're the one who always tells me to go after what I want." She leaned forward, chin on her knees with her arms wrapped around her legs.

"Are you just going to sit there?"

"Yeah."

He recognized the stubborn set to her chin—he saw it in the mirror himself. He had to remember to apologize to his parents. Knowing Madison wouldn't budge until he made the call, he pulled up Lola's number and pressed call.

She answered on the third ring. "If this is for a booty call, it's not a good time. I'm right in the middle of sex."

"I bet he's not as good as me."

She sighed. "He's really not."

He couldn't help grinning like a loon.

Madison nudged his foot. "Ask," she mouthed.

It was his turn to roll his eyes. "I have an annoying prepubescent girl here who's insisting that I ask you to a thing I have to go to on Friday."

"It's a dance," Madison yelled.

Lola laughed. "She wants you to take me to a dance?"

"It's a benefit the station is sponsoring for a homeless charity. Madison insists you'd love to put on a party dress and attend with me."

There was a pause, then Lola said in her sexy low voice, "What do you want, Sam?"

You. He glanced at his daughter, who waited eagerly. "Out, Madison."

Sighing, she flounced up. "Bye, Lola," she yelled, leaving the room.

Sam waited until Madison was out of hearing range. Then, because he knew Lola would catch his meaning, he softly said, "I'd very much like you to come."

Her breath caught. "Naughty."

"Will you go with me?"

"Yes. And then you'll come with me," she promised.

"I can't wait," he said fervently.

She laughed and hung up.

He dropped the phone on the couch and went to tell his daughter.

Madison ran out of her bedroom the moment she heard his footsteps. "She said yes?"

"Yes."

"Yay!" She hopped up and down and grabbed his hand. "We have to figure out what you're going to wear."

"I'll wear clothes." He let her drag him down the hall to his bedroom. "Besides, it's days away."

"Like only four." She shook her head like he was impossible and led him to the closet. Throwing the door open, she looked around, shoving things aside dismissively until she found a sports coat she liked. "This, with a white shirt. You look good in white. And jeans. But with nice shoes."

He watched as she got onto her hands and knees, crawling on the floor. She held up a pair triumphantly. "These."

They were the most expensive shoes he owned, a pair he'd splurged on before he blew his knee out. "Okay."

"Promise."

"I promise."

She pointed at him. "You'll text me a picture?"

"When did you become so militant?"

"This is important, Daddy."

"Okay, fine." He drew her out of the closet. "But now it's time for bed."

"Okay." She skipped to her bedroom, completely complacent now that she'd gotten what she wanted.

Shaking his head, he followed. He tucked her into her bed and turned off the light. Like every night he'd been with her since she'd been born, he rubbed her back lightly to help her calm down. He loved this part of their ritual. He felt her heart beat under her thin ribs and he swore his beat in tune.

"I'm happy you asked Lola, Daddy," his daughter murmured.

"Why do you like her so much?" he asked. He'd wondered. Madison had never pushed him toward a woman before. In fact, she'd been bratty to a couple of his ex-girlfriends in the past.

"You like her," she said now. "I could tell on the radio. You talked to her like you talk to me, and you never do that."

Madison wiggled, hugging her pillow, falling asleep a moment later.

Sam sat there in the echo of her words. From the mouths of babes.

Chapter Thirteen

LOLA BURST INTO The Sunrise Care Home, eager to share her story with her mom. She'd started over after all. She only had three weeks, but the new plotline hit her suddenly and the story was finally pouring out of her.

She thought it was good.

But her mom was the real litmus test. Lola couldn't wait to run it by her. She jogged up the stairs and to the nurses' station. "Hi, Letty. How are things?"

"Great." Letty beamed. "The inhaler did its job and the congestion in your mom's chest is clearing up. The doctor was really pleased. And today is a good day."

"How good?"

"She even recognized me."

Lola wilted against the station, joy filling her chest. Good days were few and far between—fewer and further than ever before. The last time her mother recognized her was a year ago, and it'd been so fleeting. "I'm afraid to even hope."

"I know." The nurse patted her hand. "It really sucks, doesn't it?"

"That pretty much sums it up." Lola smiled and continued down the hall. She knocked on the door and then popped her head in. "Mom?"

Sally looked up from her usual seat in the window, where she was knitting. Then she brightened. "Lola. It's been such a long time. Come in, honey."

The tightness in Lola's chest loosened, and she rushed forward to hug her mom. "Mom, it's so *nice* to see you."

Her mom held her at arm's length. "I feel like it's been a long time since I've seen you. You look different."

"How?"

"A little wiser around the edges." She frowned. "It's been a while since I've been lucid, hasn't it?"

"A little while," she conceded, not wanting to lie to her mom.

Sally cupped Lola's face, sorrow etched in every line. "I'm so sorry to be a burden, my love. You should leave me here and forget about me."

"I'd never leave you, Mom." She kissed her mom's forehead, breathing in her scent. She closed her eyes and gave a prayer of thanks for this one moment. She was very conscious of the fact that it could very well be the last lucid moment her mother ever had.

She'd cherish every second.

Swallowing back the sadness, she straightened, smiling brightly. "I have a new story to read you, Mom."

"Is it one of your books?" she said, setting aside her knitting.

"Yes. The heroine's name if Louise."

"Which bears a great resemblance to Lola." Her mother smiled fondly. "Your first story was about your father and me, so can I assume this one is about you?"

Mom remembered. Lola couldn't speak for a moment, she was so overcome. Finally, she managed to nod. "Yes, this one's about me."

"Read it to me then."

She took out the pages she'd printed and began reading the new story.

The first time she saw Sawyer, she thought he was a cretin—a cretin who kissed like he wanted to burrow deep into her and never leave. It wasn't long before Louise realized she was wrong about the cretin part, but not about him wanting her, body and soul.

She read the story about a writer and a cantankerous TV personality who was bitter about the cards dealt to him but who had a heart of gold. Whenever her mom laughed, she felt such a sense of pride that she'd willingly go through Kevin all over again just so she could appreciate her courtship with Sam that much more.

"Is that all you have?" her mother asked when she finally stopped.

"That's all I've written so far. I had to scrap the story I was writing and start over."

"I like Sawyer." Her mother nodded once to reinforce her declaration. "What's his real name?"

"Sam."

"That's a nice, solid name. He's good to you?"

"We aren't really together, Mom. We're just sniffing around each other. But we have a date tonight."

"If he was hurt before in reality like he was in your story, then of course he's going to be cautious. You just be yourself, and you'll win him over." Her mother picked up her knitting and began working at

it again.

Lola watched, admiring her manual dexterity and wondering why that wasn't affected when her mental dexterity had been. "Mom, I've been meaning to ask what you're working on. Is it a scarf?"

Her mom didn't look up looked up, as if she didn't hear the question.

"Mom?" She leaned in and touched her arm.

Sally startled, flinching back. The fear in her eyes clouded into a glazed distance, unseeing even though her hands still moved the needles.

Her mom was gone again.

Lola's heart sank, but she ruthlessly pushed back the tears. She kissed her mom's forehead and slowly put her things away. When she felt ready, she pasted a smile on her face and stood up. "I'll go now, Mom, but I'll be back Sunday to see you."

There was no reply.

Lola let herself out of the room, telling herself she wouldn't be disappointed or sad, because the few moments her mother recognized her were a gift. Lifting her head, she strode out and headed home. The best thing she could do for her mom was to have a good time tonight with Sam at his benefit.

She went home. A bath would help shake off the funk.

Because she couldn't help herself, before she went in for her bath, she checked her email. There was the usual spam, some fan mail, an email from Kevin (which she deleted), and one from Madison Taylor.

Curious didn't even begin to describe how she felt, but then she saw the subject line and stalled. *Your date with my dad.* Maybe she shouldn't open it.

Who was she kidding? Of course she was going to read it. She clicked on the email.

To: Lola Carmichael <lola@lolacarmichael.com>
From: Madison Taylor <mad_tee@hotmail.com>
Subject: Your date with my dad.

Hi Lola! Remember me? It's Madison, Sam's daughter.

You and my dad are going on a date tonight, and I just wanted to make sure you wore something really pretty, like for prom. I know I should have emailed you sooner, but my mom grounded me from

the Internet this week because I was facebooking instead of doing the dishes. Like dishes can't wait.

I hope you have something to wear.

Sincerely,
Madison

Lola couldn't help grinning as she reread the email. Apparently, Sam hadn't been kidding when he'd said Madison was harassing him to ask her out. Having the girl's blessing to date her dad had to be a good thing, right?

Something pretty... She'd had a black dress in mind, but now she had the urge to spice things up, and she knew just the dress.

She took a bath, luxuriating in the hot water until everything but the anticipation for the evening melted away. She took care to do her hair properly, blowing it out and then curling it with a brush until it was bouncy and shiny. She put on the raciest black underwear she had, wishing she'd stopped by Olivia's for something truly special. Oh well—next time. And then she slipped on her sassy red dress, completing the outfit with silver strappy shoes and chunky silver earrings she'd bought from a modern art store in New York.

She looked in the mirror and smiled. Sam was going to swallow his tongue.

Chapter Fourteen

SAM WAITED FOR Lola to answer her door. Nervous. He felt like he was a teenager again, picking up a girl he liked a lot for a first date. He stuck his hands in his pockets and hoped she wouldn't make him wait too long.

She opened the door. "You're amazingly punctual."

"And you're *smokin'*." The red dress wrapped around her neck, clingy on top, and bared a mile of creamy legs.

She ran her hands down the skirt. "Madison told me to dress like prom, but for my prom I wore a hoop dress with lace up to my neck."

He looked at her lovely neck and gave a silent prayer in thanks for it being exposed. "You're missing one thing."

"What?"

He leaned and placed a kiss on her collarbone.

He heard her soft sigh and smiled. Tonight was going to be so much better than he'd imagined. He held out his hand. "Ready to go?"

"Let's do it." She put her hand in his.

He kept her hand the whole way. She told him that she decided to start over on the book she had due, but that her new plot was so much better it was practically writing itself. He told her about the guests he had on his show that week, particularly about the sex therapist on Wednesday night who wanted to teach him tantric breathing.

As they strolled into City Hall, where the benefit was, he demonstrated the enthusiastic wheezing the therapist had taught him.

Lola laughed. "If you did that during sex, I'd die."

"That's not what's supposed to happen," he said, guiding her toward the bar set up on one side. "She assured me it'd augment my sexual interaction and make orgasms more satisfactory."

"Were your orgasms not satisfactory?"

He stopped and pulled her close. "With you, satisfactory doesn't figure on the chart. Amazing is the lowest grade."

"Don't stop." She grinned. "Tell me more."

"I'd rather show you."

"Okay," she said softly.

He wanted to kiss her so badly, but this was a work function. So he smiled at her. "Drink?"

"Please."

They walked to the bar. He ordered a gin and tonic for her and a beer for himself. Holding their drinks, they took a slow turn around the room, looking at the displays the charity had set up.

"Touchdown!"

Sam turned to find the network heads coming at him en masse, Jennifer bringing up the rear.

Great. He pasted a smile on his face. "Good to see all of you," he lied.

"Great job you're doing in the eight o'clock time slot." Owen Pickering, the president, nodded, dollar signs big and bright in his eyes. "Ratings are skyrocketing, just like Jennifer said they would."

"Jennifer's a smart lady." And he meant it, even if she'd messed with his career. But if she hadn't, he wouldn't have met Lola, so maybe being a DJ to the lovelorn wasn't such a bad thing. Call him crazy, but he was enjoying it. He wouldn't want to do it forever, but it was an interesting change of perspective.

"Thanks, Sam." Suspicion laced the edges of Jennifer's smile. Then she turned to Lola. "This is a surprise, Ms. Carmichael."

"Please call me Lola."

Jennifer turned to the execs. "Lola Carmichael is a bestselling author and Sam's first guest."

One of the other men cooed. "Then the show was obviously good for *your* love life, eh, Touchdown?"

"Maybe we should market that," one of the other men said.

"My private life is private," Sam declared before they went too far down that road. "There will be no marketing it."

"We'll see." Pickering clapped him on the shoulder and walked away, his entourage trailing after him.

Except for Jennifer, who was looking at Lola curiously.

He was no stranger to the cattiness of women. He braced himself for the bitchy comment that'd mess things up for him with Lola. He didn't want things with Lola to go bad. In fact, he wanted just the opposite.

He liked her. A whole lot.

Jennifer was asking Lola about her current

project, which Lola was answering vaguely when some woman rushed up to them. "Lola Carmichael!"

His date smiled warmly. "Jane, what a surprise. It's so great to see you."

The woman air-kissed Lola's cheeks. "You'll never guess who's here. *Kali Singh*. Remember, the columnist for Cosmo? You *have* to come say hello. Can I borrow Lola for a second? I'll bring her right back."

Before Sam could say anything, the woman dragged his date away. Looking over her shoulder, Lola shot him an apologetic smile. He nodded, letting her know it was fine—that she should do what she needed to do.

He and Jennifer watched her go.

"I didn't think it was possible," Jennifer said.

"What?" He sipped his beer.

"That you could actually care about a woman." She shook her head. "I thought hell would freeze over before I saw the day you looked at a woman like that."

"Like what?" he asked cautiously.

"Like you want to devour her, of course, but also like you're ready to tear apart anyone who got too close to her."

Did he look like that? "Does this mean I get my old show back?"

"Of course not." Jennifer looked at him like he was insane. "You've only known her a few days. Let's make sure it's not a fluke. Good try though."

Lola looked up at him from across the room, *help* written in her eyes. "Excuse me," he murmured to Jennifer, going to rescue to his date.

When he reached her, the two women she was with were in the middle of a discussion about some sort of art. He slipped an arm around Lola and said loudly, "I have to steal Lola away. There's a matter of romantic importance and her opinion's needed."

The two people barely glanced at him before continuing.

"Thank you." Lola heaved a sigh and leaned into him. "I thought my head was going to explode."

He held her body against his, liking how it fit there. "What were they talking about?"

"Hair art."

"Like for supermodels?" he asked as he led her from the main gallery up the large staircase.

"No. It's a type of art from the nineteenth century, where they took the hair of dead loved ones and

turned it into paintings." She made a face. "My friend Gwen told me about it."

"Creepy."

"No kidding. I'd have tried to pry myself away, but my agent's been trying to hook me up with Kali Singh forever. Being featured in her column would up sales." She looked around. "Where are we going? There's not much going on up here."

"Exactly." He guided her into a secluded alcove hidden by a curtain and turned her into his arms.

"This is the romantic emergency?" she asked, putting her arms around his neck.

"I'm dying," he whispered, kissing her lovely neck.

She arched her head back. "Do you need mouth to mouth?"

"Hell yeah." He took her lips, just like he'd been thinking about all day.

They kissed, and kissed some more, until it wasn't enough. He lifted his head and looked around. "Here," he said, leading her to the windowsill. He perched on it and drew her between his legs.

But soon that wasn't enough either—for either one of them. Lola was the one who made the next gesture, undoing his pants and pulling him out.

They both looked down at her hand holding it. Then he reached into his pocket and handed her the condom he'd brought, just in case.

She smiled like a siren as she sheathed him with it and then climbed on. Straddling him, she sighed as she slid all the way down. "We seem to get it on standing up a lot."

He untied the back of her dress, exposing a lacy black bra. "Do you mind?"

"Do I seem like I mind?"

"It's a good leg workout." He lowered one side of the bra and thumbed her nipple.

She hissed, arching into his touch. "That's exactly what I think every time we do this."

"If you're able to think, I'm not doing this right."

"You're doing okay, but you can always try harder."

"Harder I can do," he murmured against her neck, and he did just that.

Chapter Fifteen

KRISTIN ASKED EVE for a week of strategic scheduling: to work later in the mornings rather than opening. She wanted to give Rob a chance to miss her by not starting off his day with her.

Eve had asked her what'd happen if he didn't notice, but Kristin was confident he would. A man didn't kiss a woman like Rob had and then forget her.

Monday, she resumed her normal schedule. She toyed with the idea of looking especially nice for when she saw him, but she didn't want him to have unreasonable expectations of what he was getting.

Like clockwork, Rob came in for coffee and pastries before work, Chanel trotting alongside him.

Kristin felt a tingle of excitement at the way he smoldered at her as he stalked toward the counter. She wanted to crawl across the top and meet him halfway for another one of those explosive kisses.

But instead she tipped her head and gave him a knowing smile to remind him how sassy her lips could be. "Hi."

"Where have you been?"

She poured him coffee. "Did you miss me?"

He looked her over like he wanted to drizzle chocolate on her and lick her clean. "I have a proposition for you."

"The answer is yes."

A smile touched his lips. "You don't know what it is."

"No, but I can hope."

"I have something I need help with. You're the perfect person for it."

"Am I?" she asked softly.

"Yes," he said confidently. "Maybe we could get together later today to discuss the details? Over dinner."

She loved the idea of a date. "That'd be great."

"Remember where I live?" When she nodded, he said, "Come over around seven."

"I'll be there."

He smoldered at her all the way out the door. She waited till she couldn't see him to thrust a fist in the air. "*Yes*."

It wasn't until later that she noticed they'd both forgotten about his coffee and pastry. Oh well—she'd give him something even more delicious and sweet later.

Kristin arrived at Rob's a few minutes late, because she went home to wash the coffee smell out of her hair and change into sexier clothes. Ready, she rang the doorbell.

He opened the door, delicious in his dress shirt with its sleeves rolled up and unbuttoned at the collar. He smiled at her, looking her over in a way that sent tingles up and down her body. "Come in."

Her goal had been a sperm donor—she hadn't been optimistic about finding anyone to share her life. Even if she set aside the fact that she had too much money, she wasn't an easy person to live with. She'd been on her own too long—she was too set in her ways.

But there was something about Rob. With him, she felt like it could work, and her gut reactions had never led her astray.

The puppy ran up to greet her. Kneeling, Kristin

scratched it in all usual places. "Hey there, Chanel."

The dog woofed once and then trotted away, obviously satisfied with the attention.

"What did the vet say?"

"He gave her a clean bill of health," Rob assured her. "He was impressed, given she was a stray."

"She's an impressive dog."

"I think so. Come this way." Rob led her down the hall.

She started to tell him she remembered the way to the study, but then he veered and led her into the dining room. She paused in the doorway, not liking the room for its coldness and formality. She wanted to ask him if they could move to the floor in his study, but all the documents on the table confused her. "What is all this?"

"What I wanted to talk to you about. Sit." He pulled out a chair for her and then took the one across from her.

Too far away. She almost moved to the seat next to him, but then a database schema on the table right in front of her caught her eye. Picking it up, she slowly sat down. "This is for one of your stock databases?"

"Yes. It doesn't perform the way we'd optimally

like, and I haven't found the right person to fix it. But I have a feeling you might be the right person."

Frowning, she stared at the paper. "In what way?"

He began to describe what he used the database for and how it fell short of what he needed. The augmentations he wanted were a piece of cake—a junior database admin could accomplish them.

Except he was asking her to do them.

She liked that he thought she was The One, but she'd have preferred if it wasn't because of her tech knowledge. She'd left that world behind.

But it wouldn't take much to do what he wanted. It was easy for her, and it'd benefit him. She'd look at this like a test. If she passed it, she was in. He was trusting her with his business, and she knew for a man like him that meant a lot. He didn't think their worlds were compatible, and this was her chance to show how well-matched they really were.

So she focused and asked him a few more questions about how he and his team used the database.

At first, Rob looked startled but then he answered her eagerly.

She made some notes and then considered the

work. It wasn't hard, but she'd have to work on it at night, after her shifts at Grounds for Thought. And she wanted to add a couple customizable features to the interface that Rob needed in the long run. She pursed her lips, estimating. "It'll take me two weeks, maybe three."

He stared at her. "You really can do it."

"Well, yeah. I'm perfect for this. I'd have to be stupid to say I'd do it if I couldn't."

"Then why are you working at the café? There are countless tech jobs these days, especially for someone good."

"Maybe no one will hire me," she said blithely, looking down at her notes.

"You were hired at the café."

"Eve has low standards," she lied. "So are you going to feed me any time soon? Because I didn't eat lunch."

He frowned at her as he stood up. "You need to eat more regularly."

"Yes, sir." She rolled her eyes and followed him to the kitchen.

He glanced at her as he opened the refrigerator door. "I'm serious."

"I've made it thirty-eight years without major mishap. I'm pretty sure I can take care of myself."

He froze and gawked at her. "You're *thirty-eight*?"

"Yeah." She arched her brow as she hopped onto the counter. "You didn't seriously think I was eighteen or something."

"Not quite, but close." He studied her face as though searching for signs of age.

She shrugged, feeling self-conscious. "It's only genes. My mom is sixty-nine and looks like she's barely forty. How old are you?"

"Forty."

"And you're single?" She tsked. "Some people would wonder what's wrong with you."

"Aren't you single?"

"Yes, but everyone knows what's wrong with me."

"And what's that?" he asked as he set a tray of lasagna in the microwave.

"I do my own thing. Men can't handle that."

"Some men can."

She didn't care about some men—she cared about him. "You like independent women?"

"Yes." He leaned against the counter. "I work a

lot of hours, and most women don't understand that. They want someone who'll be around more."

"Are you planning to work as much when you have a family?"

"I guess I'll cross that bridge when I get to it."

"If we had a family together, you'd have to be available."

"Since when are we having a family together?"

Since always. "It's non-negotiable, by the way. Our kid doesn't need an absentee father."

"I wouldn't be an absentee father." He checked on the lasagna, taking it out of the microwave and setting it on the counter. "My dad was always around. I know how important that is."

"My dad was always around too." She opened a drawers until she found the silverware. Taking two forks, she handed one to Rob before leaning on the counter and digging straight into the pan. Why dirty dishes if you didn't have to?

She knew Rob stared at her, but then he followed her lead.

"For the record," she said around a hot bite of pasta, "I'm staying at home once the kids are born."

"Kids?"

"Homer and Ulysses." She shrugged at his questioning look. "Start them off on a great note, don't you think?"

"Or else spend a fortune on therapy when they're picked on constantly in school."

She fed him a nicely crusted piece. "I know it's very un-PC to be a stay-at-home mom, but I don't want to miss any part of them growing up."

"I'll miss seeing your face in the mornings at the café," he admitted.

"You won't miss my face, because I'll be waking up with you every morning." She grinned at him. "You'll see more than my face."

He shook his head. "You need to stop talking like that."

"Like what?" She batted her eyelashes innocently.

"I meant it when I said that I don't fool around with people who work for me."

Kristin dropped her fork. "You mean that while I'm revamping your database, there's not going to be any monkey business?"

"Exactly."

"You're going to miss kissing me, you know."

His gaze fell to her lips, which she licked to punctuate her point. "Most likely," he conceded.

"You're going to miss touching me, too." She set her fork down and trapped him against the counter, pressing herself flush against him. "We feel perfect, touching body-to-body like this. You can't deny that."

"No, I can't." He held her close, his fingers running up her back.

Sighing, she arched into his caress. If only he'd do more, or slide his hands under her shirt. "But you still insist on this no fraternization policy?"

"Yes." He sounded torn, like he could be swayed.

Maybe she should get someone else to do the work for him. She knew plenty of people who were qualified. She could pass it along and manage the job to make sure it was done properly.

But she wanted to show him that she was on his side, that he could trust her—what better way than showing him she understood what he needed? The moratorium on their relationship would only incentivize her to get the work done sooner. Everyone would come out ahead in the end.

"Okay." She stepped away and stuck her hand out. "Deal."

He blinked as though startled and stared at her

hand like he didn't understand what it meant. Then he shook his head and took her hand. "Good."

The warm glide of his palm against hers made her shiver, and she vowed this was going to be the shortest term consulting gig in the history of tech, because she wanted to feel that palm slide all over her body and she wasn't taking no for an answer.

Chapter Sixteen

LOLA HUNCHED OVER her laptop, tapping furiously at the keyboard. After all those fits and false starts, the book was shaping up. The words were literally pouring out of her in an unstoppable whirlwind.

She usually worried about the quality of her writing, but she had a giddy feeling that this was the best thing she'd ever written. The pacing was brisk, the dialogue was snappy, and the characters were awesome. Louise and Sawyer fairly sizzled on the page.

Not as much as she and Sam sizzled in real life, but it was close.

Of course, she didn't write *everything* she and Sam did. No one would believe how great the reality was.

Her gaze drifted out the window as she remembered the private after-party they'd had the night of the benefit. They'd eventually made it back to her apartment where they'd stayed up all night talking—and other stuff—finally falling asleep in the early morning hours. He'd stayed Saturday, leaving Sunday morning only because he was scheduled to pick up his daughter.

She sighed happily. It'd been a *nice* weekend.

Lola usually didn't like having someone around while she was working. Kevin used to disrupt her writing all the time, asking her questions and generally demanding her attention.

Sam went out to the car to get his gym bag and came back with a latte for her. A couple hours later, when she came up for air, he made her a salad and sent her off to work more, sitting on the couch in her living room and reading.

Clarification: reading *her* book.

When she'd noticed it, she stalled for a moment, oddly touched. She'd never cared if anyone she knew read her work as long as they bought a copy to support her. Romance wasn't everyone's cup of tea, especially a manly man like Touchdown Taylor.

But she'd watched him as he read it, and she could tell he enjoyed it by the little smile on his face. Every now and then he'd burst out laughing, and her

heart turned over.

It did a lot of that around him.

Her phone rang. Speak of the devil, she thought when she looked at the screen. She answered it.

"I need a huge favor," he said without preamble. "My ex-wife decided to drop Madison off without warning, so I don't have a babysitter lined up for her, but I have to go to work. I know you've got to write, but do you think you could come over and do it here?"

"You want me to take care of Madison?"

"I know. It's asking a lot."

"No, I'm just surprised because I got the impression you don't trust her with just anyone."

"That's why I called you."

Her heart did that funny flopping thing again. "When do you need me over?"

"Five minutes ago."

She chuckled. "I'm on my way."

Scribbling down the address he gave her, she packed up her laptop and notes and went to rescue him.

The address belonged to a large flat in the lower Haight. The outside of the building was a bit rundown. She rang the doorbell and a moment later she heard heavy footsteps jogging down stairs and the door opened.

"Thank you," he said fervently, drawing her inside and kissing her quickly. "I owe you. Big time. I'm sorry. I need to go. I'm late."

"Go. We'll be fine," she said, even though she didn't have the slightest idea of what to do with an eleven year old. Being an only child, she'd never had to babysit.

He kissed her again. "I'll be home after ten. Madison should be in bed by nine."

"Go." She smiled after him as he ran out and then closed the door. Walking up the flight of stairs to the flat, she called out, "Madison?"

"In here," came her little voice from the front of the apartment.

She headed toward it, peeking into the various rooms along the way. She'd expected a man cave—all dark colors and messy. It wasn't obsessively clean, but neither was it slovenly. She'd call it homey, with lived in furniture and photos of Madison all over as well as pictures of various other people she decided were relatives based on their resemblances.

In the living room, Madison sat on the floor at the coffee table, frowning at a blank piece of paper. She looked up, her expression sour. "I hate writing essays."

"What do you have to write about?" She sat on the floor across from the girl.

"Christopher Columbus. I have to explain how his explorations affected the new world."

Lola made a face. "Yuck."

"I know."

She thought about it for a moment. If she had to write it, she'd do it in narrative instead of essay form. "Do you like stories?"

"I love to read."

"Then why don't you write a story instead of a strict essay? If it were me, I'd write from the point of view of an indigenous person who was invaded by Columbus and his men. Make sure you include the points you're supposed to address."

Madison blinked. "You think that'd be okay?"

She shrugged. "It depends on your teacher, but if you don't take a chance, you won't know. You could get extra points for creativity."

"I'm going to do it." She tapped her pencil against

her nose a few times and then lit into the paper.

Lola got out her laptop and wrote too, but about a different type of conquering that involved velvety, moist spots.

An hour later, Madison held up her pages triumphantly. "I've got my first draft, and it's awesome."

"Good." Lola closed the lid on her laptop. "Because it's past your bedtime."

The girl pouted. "I'm not sleepy though."

Lola didn't want to be an ogre, but she didn't want to be a pushover either. So she said, "Get ready for bed and maybe we can watch part of a movie in bed on my laptop."

"Okay." Madison jumped up eagerly and ran off.

Lola followed more slowly, straightening up a little on the way. By the time she found Madison's room in the back, the girl was in her pjs and climbing in bed.

She looked around the room, impressed. Sam had done a nice job of giving his daughter a space of her own. She could see Madison's personality in the superhero posters and the furry white bedspread and rug. "Your room is great."

"I know, right?" She pulled the covers up to her

chest. "Daddy said I could do whatever I wanted. Within reason."

Lola grinned at what was obviously Sam's lingo. "What was outside reason?"

"Black walls." The girl shrugged. "It'd have looked cool."

Lola settled on the bed next to Madison, leaning against the headboard. "What type of movies do you like?"

"Action movies. And westerns." At Lola's questioning look, the girl shrugged. "My dad likes them."

"I like dance movies. Have you ever seen *Step Up*, or *Step Up 2*?"

Madison shook her head.

Her mouth dropped open in exaggerated shock. "What? How about *Footloose*? The remake of course."

"No."

"*Dirty Dancing*?"

"No."

"Oh my God. I'm going to have to speak to your father about your lack of education on this." She opened her laptop and pulled up her movie directory. "*Dirty Dancing* is a classic, but we don't have enough time to watch it."

"A classic like Butch Cassidy and the Sundance Kid?" At Lola's questioning look, Madison just said, "That's one of Daddy's favorite movies."

"Figures." She opened the file. "You have to watch *Dirty Dancing* all the way through, beginning to end, so we'll do that another night. But we can watch a couple dance snippets from *Step Up 2*. Like the beginning on the subway, the club scene, and the end, I think."

She'd watched them so many times she found the scenes without any trouble. The story lines in the *Step Up* movies weren't the highest quality, but the dance sequences and the music were great.

As soon as it started, her foot began to tap. Just like always when she watched them—and she watched them often—she felt like hopping up and trying out the moves herself, even if she knew she'd look ridiculous.

By the end of the third scene, Madison was on her knees, avidly watching and just as excited.

Good girl, Lola thought fondly.

The girl groaned in disappointment when Lola closed her laptop. "Let's watch them again. That was awesome."

"How about if we make a movie date? You guys can come over and we'll torture your dad with them."

Madison giggled. "Okay."

"Bedtime?"

"I'll just read a little." She picked up a book from the bedside table and crawled into bed. "Will you tuck me in?"

Lola's heart flopped. She'd never seen herself as a mom, but this she could do. She tucked Madison under the covers and ran a hand over her hair. "I'll be in the living room if you need me."

"Okay." The girl was already engrossed in reading. Right before Lola walked out, Madison said, "Tonight was fun, Lola. I'm glad you were here."

"Me too," she said softly and closed the door behind her.

Sam came home to a still house.

The light was on in the living room. He peeked in, finding Lola asleep on the couch, her laptop still open on her legs.

He liked seeing her there. It made his chest fill with a warmth he hadn't felt—well, ever, really.

Not wanting to analyze it, he went back to check on Madison. She'd fallen asleep with the lights on, a book her hand—typical for her. He set the book aside and kissed her forehead before turning off her light and returning to Lola.

She was sleeping so peacefully, he didn't want to disturb her. But as he lifted the computer from her lap, she stirred. "Sam?"

He sat on the couch and gathered her into his arms, so she snuggled half on top of him. "Was everything okay tonight? Madison didn't give you trouble?"

She looked up with a sleepy frown. "I can't believe you've never shown her *Dirty Dancing*."

Stroking her hair, he grinned. "That's what you took away from the evening?"

"That and that you really are a cowboy."

"What?"

"Nothing."

He shrugged. Maybe she was still dreaming. "Did you get any work done, or did I totally disrupt your night."

"I wrote a chapter, actually." She yawned and burrowed her head closer. "Madison had homework,

so we wrote together. She's a good kid, Sam."

She really was. "She's inconvenient at the moment though."

"How so?" Lola asked, looking at him.

He stroked her hair. "I'd like nothing better than to carry you to my bed, undress you, and make slow, passionate love to you. But I can't with Madison in the room next door."

"This is the part where I'm supposed to say it's just as nice snuggling on the couch and talking with you, but that'd be a lot of crap." She ran her hand inside the collar of his shirt. "I'd rather be naked in bed with you, too."

"Next time," he promised.

She smiled up at him. "Very soon."

Chapter Seventeen

It was super late. Not quite midnight, Kristin saw on her laptop's clock. Way too late to call Rob, especially since he woke up so early.

She still wanted to.

It'd probably just go to voicemail. He seemed like the sensible type who'd silence his phone when he went to sleep so he wouldn't be disturbed.

She looked at her computer screen. She *did* have a question to ask him about his database. But really, she just wanted to hear his voice. It'd been a few days since they had that "business meeting" in his dining room, and she missed him. She hadn't even gotten to flirt with him when he came in for his morning coffee because she'd been scheduled for the afternoon shift.

Grabbing her phone, she called the number he'd given her. She waited, expecting it to go directly to voicemail.

"Hello?"

She blinked. "Rob?"

"Kristin?" There was a frown in his tired voice. "Are you okay?"

"I'm great. What are you doing up? I was going to leave a message."

"Do you want me to hang up?"

She grinned at the humor in his voice. "That's okay. I'll just ask you in person. Unless you're trying to sleep."

"To be honest, I'm having trouble falling asleep."

She heard a rustle. Sheets? Was he in bed? She pictured him there, stretching under the covers. "Do you wear pajamas?"

"Excuse me?"

"Do you wear pajamas to bed?" she repeated.

"Why? Do you think that's why I can't fall asleep?"

"We could take them off and find out."

He paused. For a moment she thought he was going to tell her she stepped over some line, but she was so happy when he said, "I've never been sexually harassed by someone working for me."

"I'm glad I'm a first." She closed her laptop. "You

know what helps when you can't sleep?"

"What?"

"Sex. But maybe we should start off slower, like with a walk."

"Right now?"

"Well, yeah." She reached for her flip-flops. "I'll meet you in front of the Ferry Building in fifteen."

She'd expected him to make excuses, but he surprised her by saying, "See you there."

She was already on her feet. She wouldn't bother changing out of her pajamas—he might as well see her in her natural state—but her hair was a mess. She redid her ponytail and then swiped gloss onto her lips to make them shiny and inviting.

Grabbing a hoodie and a scarf, she ran out of her house and to her car. She didn't drive much because public transportation was easier than parking in the city, but at this time of night in her neighborhood there were no buses, and it'd take at least half an hour for a cab to arrive.

She parked her Porsche a couple blocks away, far enough so Rob wouldn't see her in with it. It was a short walk up Embarcadero to the Ferry Building, where he leaned against a column, waiting for her.

Her girlie parts began to party, and that voice inside sighed and said, *Yes, HIM*.

She wanted to run up to him and throw her arms around him, to kiss the bejesus out of him, but she knew how he felt about fraternizing with the help, so she planned on behaving herself as long as she was "working" for him.

So she sauntered up with a saucy grin. "Ready for the sleep remedy?"

"Do I need to brace myself?" he asked as he fell into step beside her.

"I'm breaking you in gently. This usually works for mild cases of insomnia."

"You have trouble sleeping, too, then?"

Not since she quit working at Aspire. "I used to."

"And whatever we're doing worked best?"

"We're walking briskly, but no, the best remedy is hot, sweaty sex." She gauged his reaction. He was thinking about it—imagining it. Good, because she imagined it a lot, and why should he be exempt from the torture? "We'll try that next, if we need to resort to drastic measures."

"I can't."

"You can't have sex?" She dropped her gaze to his crotch.

"*No.*" He scowled at her. "Not that."

"Oh, good." She heaved a sigh of relief. "Because that'd have made me sad."

"Think how it'd make me." He shook his head. "I can't have sex with you. You're working for me. I told you that already."

"I'm just doing one little tech thing, and that'll be over soon." Then watch out.

"You're working for me," he insisted, "and I never overstep the employer-employee boundary."

"You've never dated anyone you've worked with?" she asked curiously.

"No."

She hadn't either, but she'd know plenty of her executive team who'd broken that taboo. It never turned out well, and there were plenty of fish outside the work tank. "I like that you're principled, even if it puts a temporary dent in my plans."

"What plans?"

"To seduce you."

He kept pace with her, but his expression was intent, like he was trying to cipher her out. Then, thoughtfully, he said, "What would you do?"

She blinked. "Excuse me?"

"To seduce me. What would you do?"

The intensity of his gaze made her catch her breath. She felt the pull of his body and wanted to touch him, but she managed to resist. She didn't trust herself not to mess the moment up.

Besides, not touching him was turning her on. She could see he wanted her, that *he* was picturing touching her, and that was almost as good as the real thing.

"Well?" he prompted, his voice low with desire.

"Maybe I'd tie you up," she said recklessly. "I'd wait for you to come home from work and slip your tie right off your neck and use it to bind your hands."

He didn't say anything.

Didn't he like that? Having him at her mercy seemed pretty hot to her. She pictured kissing him all over and knew her labored breathing wasn't from their brisk pace.

"That's the wrong picture."

She startled out of her erotic dream. "How do you know what I was picturing?"

He gave her a baleful look. "You're the one who'd be tied up, although I have a feeling it'd take more than one tie to keep you still."

"So are you offering?"

"No. You're working for me," he repeated.

"And you don't tie up people who work for you. I know." She held up a hand. "But I'm almost done. *Then* you can tie me up. I give you permission."

"You're not like anyone I've ever met."

"In a good way, I hope."

They walked in silence. She could tell he was thinking, and she let him. Until she saw a bench at the end of a pier. Unable to help herself, she took his hand. "This way."

He clasped it, caressing her fingers with his thumb.

She pretended to goggle at him. "Hand-holding doesn't break your moral code?"

"It should." He didn't let go.

Warmth flooded her. He liked her, too. This was going to work out. She'd finish his database project and then he'd see that she had his back and wanted to share his life, and then they could have lots of sex and babies.

They reached the end of the pier and sat on the bench. The wind whipped through her, and she scooted closer to him for warmth.

"You need another layer," he said, taking off the scarf around his neck and wrapping it around hers.

His scent enveloped her, and she inhaled it, wanting to remember it forever.

Out of the blue, Rob asked, "Do you ever want more than what you have?"

She shook her head. "I have so much."

He looked at her, confusion lining his face.

She couldn't blame him. To him, she was a destitute barista instead of a former tech mogul with more money than Croesus. Frankly, there was only one thing she lacked. "I want a baby," she admitted.

"That surprises me. I wouldn't have guessed that from you."

"What? I don't seem maternal?"

"That's not it." He studied her.

"And now you're thinking that I'm getting too old to have children." She glared at him. "Yes, children, because I'd have three if I could, but at this point I'd take just one. I won't be greedy."

"I wasn't thinking you were getting old. You barely look thirty."

"My eggs are two hundred sixty-six in dog years."

They sat in silence until he said, "Why haven't

you had a child by now if it's so important?"

"Because I didn't realize how important it was until recently." Until she'd realized she wasn't happy working eighty hours a week and that she wanted to create something really important for once—something, or someone, who could change the future instead of just make rich men richer. "But I have a plan."

Rob smiled. "I'm both curious and frightened to know what that is."

"Because you're a wise man." She looked up at him. His lips were so close—it wouldn't take anything to kiss him.

She wanted to so badly.

He wanted it, too—she could tell by the way he returned her gaze with unwavering heat. He brushed a strand of hair from her face, his thumb a soft rasp on her skin.

He leaned toward her...

And she jerked back. Rob had his principles, and she didn't want to compromise them and have him resent her. So she stood up. "You should go to bed."

He stood up with her, standing so close his body's gravity tugged at hers, making her waver. "What about you?" he asked.

"Are you inviting me?" she joked.

He touched her lips with a finger. "You don't know how tempting that is."

YES, HIM, her hormones screamed at her. And she wanted it. She wanted it more than she'd ever wanted anything.

Which was why she stepped away and said, "Take me home?"

He looked surprised, but he didn't try to change her mind. Good thing, because she'd have caved in a second if he'd pressed the issue. But she had to think of the big picture, and a one-night stand wasn't beneficial.

So she walked with him to his car and let him drive her home, and he held her hand the whole way.

It made having to cab back to fetch her car later so totally worth it.

Chapter Eighteen

"SAM?" SOMEONE KNOCKED on the doorframe to the studio.

He looked up to find Jennifer peering into the room.

"Just wanted to let you know the ratings from last night were off the charts." She smiled like a happy shark. "Good job."

"Thanks to you." He'd expected the relationship counselor she'd booked to be boring, but the man had actually been entertaining. They'd exchanged good, veiled banter, and after the show the guy had given him his card and invited him out for a drink. It was San Francisco, after all. Sam had just thanked him and told him his attention was otherwise engaged.

"You've actually done a good job with this segment, Sam," Jennifer said in wonder.

"Don't sound so surprised."

"Frankly, I'm shocked. I didn't think your ego could take it."

"I hadn't either." He'd thought this show would be all fluff and no substance. But then he'd started to get fan mail where women told him his unique perspective on life and love helped them change their lives for the better.

It was oddly touching.

Not that he didn't want to go back to his sports show, but he wasn't in as much of a hurry.

Who'd have thought?

"I knew love would be good for you. Meaning Lola," Jennifer clarified unnecessarily.

It was an immediate reaction to deny it, but he couldn't. More surprisingly, he didn't want to.

Jennifer smirked at him. "No comment? No denial."

"Not at all," he replied without hesitation.

Gawking at him in wonder, she shook her head. "Who'd have thought a tiger could change his stripes? Come in early on Monday. I want to talk to you."

"Why?" he asked suspiciously.

"To discuss returning you to your old show."

Triumph flared in his chest, but he didn't let it

show. He leaned back in his chair, arms folded behind his head. "Only if I can stay on and do *Ladies' Night* once a week."

"Deal," Jennifer said instantly, and then scurried down the hall before he could say another word, her heels a satisfied staccato on the tiles.

He grinned. Life was good.

He returned his attention to his lineup for the evening. Jennifer's team had set up an author who'd written a book on dating.

There was another knock, and an intern popped his head in. "Your wife is on line two."

Lola? Sam perked up, until he realized that she wouldn't call herself his wife. The fact that he thought she might showed how far gone he was. He smiled mockingly at himself. "I'm not married. Maybe it's for someone else."

"No, she said you specifically." The college boy frowned in confusion. "Her name is Chelsea?"

Hell. He was tempted to tell the intern to field the call, but not only couldn't he do that to him but there was the possibility Chelsea was cutting out on Madison again, and Sam didn't want to leave his daughter uncared for. So he picked up the line. "Chelsea?"

"How dare you bring your floozies around Madison?" Her voice was ice, and he could imagine the matching look in her eyes. He'd plenty of experience with it.

He debated how to handle this. He wanted to poke at her, but that wouldn't help Madison, so he chose calm instead. "Chelsea, I have my show in a few minutes. I'm happy to let you finish your rant, but it needs to be quick."

"I'm going to call my lawyer," she threatened, like usual. "I'm going to have you declared unfit so you can't taint my daughter with your loose morals."

There was no way in hell he'd allow anyone to come between him and his daughter. He waited for the urge to fire back to roll through him, but there was just calm. Strange. Usually he had to struggle to keep from strangling Chelsea.

"Don't you have anything to say?" his ex-wife snapped.

"I'm sorry, Chelsea."

"What?"

He exhaled. "I'm sorry for whatever I did to make you so bitter. I'm sorry I couldn't be what you needed."

Silence echoed heavy on the other end of the line. Then she said, "Whatever you're trying isn't going to work, you know."

"I'm not trying anything. I'm apologizing."

"Are you drunk?"

"I'm at work," he said, throwing his arms up in exasperation. "Give me a break here. I'm trying to be nice to you."

"Why?" Suspicion lay heavy on the one word.

"Because for better or worse, you're the mother of my child, and Madison is the most important thing here. Us being like this doesn't help her." He paused, wondering how far to go. But then it had to be said, so might as well get it over with. "And because the woman you called a floozy is the woman I love."

"You don't know what love is," she said bitterly.

He sighed. "I don't blame you for thinking that."

"Don't think that this means I'm just going to let Madison be around you so she can watch you make out with your girlfriend."

He gritted his teeth at the implication that he'd do anything to damage his daughter. But he knew this had nothing to do with Madison, or really even him. "Of course you wouldn't, Chelsea. You love Madison and don't want her hurt. You're a good mother."

She sputtered on the other end of the line.

He tried not to feel satisfied that he'd managed to strike her speechless, but he lost that battle. "I'm going on the air in a couple minutes. I'm happy to discuss this more if that'd make you more comfortable with the situation, but Lola is here to stay in the picture, and that's not going to change."

"Fine," she snapped with a last vestige of bitchiness and then hung up.

"That went well," he muttered as he set the phone down. Then he got his head back in the game.

His guest wasn't due to come on until halfway into the show, so he looked at the notes that he'd made about what to start off with.

The moment he was cued to go on air, he changed the game plan. "Welcome to *Ladies' Night*. As you all know, usually we talk about relationships and dating and all those thing you women love to discuss, but that makes us guys cringe." He paused, smiling. "Tonight I want to talk about a byproduct of love. Children.

"No, I'm not going to talk about making them. I want to discuss raising them, because good parenting

forms a solid base for how your child relates to his or her future partners. If you want your kid to be happy in love later, you've got to consciously teach them about love."

He paused, thinking about his own dad, who'd been absent so often. Shaking his head, he continued, "I have the most smart, beautiful, amazing daughter. One day, when she's thirty and I finally let her start dating, I hope she finds someone who'll cherish and love her the way she deserves.

"But will she recognize that? I don't know. My ex-wife and I haven't been poster children for good relationships. My daughter is eleven, going on forty-two. Have we scarred her? Is it too late for her to develop a healthy image of love? You tell me. Caller one, Jackie from Pinole."

"Hi Sam. My ex and I fought a lot, and my son grew up to marry a nice girl, but I worry that they're *too* non-confrontational. You know?"

He nodded. "As though they're on the opposite end of the spectrum?"

"Yes." She sighed. "Being a parent isn't easy. You're always worried about the example you're setting and that you're permanently scarring your child for life. They don't tell you that before you get pregnant."

Chuckling, he took the next call. "John from Livermore, you're on *Ladies' Night*."

"Sam, I gotta tell you, man, I never thought I'd call in to a girls' talk show, but you rock, man. My wife made me start to listen. She thinks I could learn a thing or two."

"Thanks, John." He leaned back. "We're chatting about kids tonight. Do you and your wife have any?"

"Two." The pride was evident in his voice. "Both girls. The estrogen in this house is frickin' suffocating. But I'd do anything for my three ladies. My dad always said you protect your own. You know what I mean."

"Yes."

"It was an eye-opener, having girls. It hit me real hard one day when I caught my oldest watch me and my wife fight. I gotta teach them how a man should treat his woman, just like my dad taught me. It's a responsibility."

"I feel you, John. Thanks for calling in and good luck with your daughters." He hung up and picked

up the next call. "We're discussing whether your parents' relationship dictates how well you relate to future mates. Elle from San Francisco, you're on *Ladies' Night*."

"This is my first time calling in, Sam, but first I wanted to tell you how I enjoy your show."

He recognized that sexy voice. It sounded like... Elle. L. *Lola*. He sat up, his whole being coming to life. "Thank you, *L*."

"I'm your biggest fan. I listen every night. It's like you're hanging out with me in my living room."

He grinned at the lilt of humor in her voice. If he were in her living room, he'd definitely be hanging out, though both of them would be naked. "What are your thoughts, *L*?"

"My parents had a happy relationship, right up until my father died. Their story was like a fairy tale, where they saw each other from across the room and got together despite all the odds." She sighed dreamily. "Now I know I was lucky to have that example, but I used to wonder if it wasn't a bad thing."

"How so?" he asked, genuinely curious.

"It made me set my sights for the unrealistic goal of finding a Prince Charming."

The urge to declare that he wanted to be her Prince Charming was shockingly strong. "And now?"

"Now I realize that it's good to have high expectations. If you don't, you might settle for less than what you deserve, just because you don't think you're worth it." She paused briefly. "Recently I met someone who takes me to the moon and back, and if I didn't have my parents' example I might not appreciate what this man gives me."

His heart beat hard in his chest. She was talking about him. He wanted to pound on his chest and crow like a caveman. But he managed to calmly say, "What does your future look like with this man?"

"It's too early to know where it's going to go, but even if it ended today I'd be forever grateful for every second with him."

"I'm sure it won't end," he said, trying to sound normal.

"It won't?" There was teasing humor in her voice. "You sense this?"

"I'm a relationship expert after all."

"I though you were Touchdown Taylor."

"What do you think my nickname means?" He grinned when she chuckled softly.

"You sound like you're a good father, Sam," Lola said on the line. "Your daughter is lucky. I'm sure you're a great example to her of how to live and love. Just like my mom was for me."

"Your mother must be happy for you."

The tenor of their connection changed instantly. Even in the brief silence, he could tell something was wrong.

Then she said, "My mom was diagnosed with early onset dementia ten years ago. She—most days, she doesn't remember me, but I think deep down she knows I'm happy, and that pleases her."

He didn't know that. Why didn't he know? He heard her pain and wanted to take her in his arms. "I'm sorry about your mother."

"I—I don't talk about it much," she said, as if hearing his silent questions. She cleared her throat. "Well, I've just brought your show down. Sorry. I'd tell a joke to get things upbeat again but I'm afraid I'd cause the rest of your audience to ditch, too."

"I doubt that. I think we all appreciate the reminder that love is fleeting, and that we should embrace every moment of it while we have it."

"Yes."

"Thanks for calling in," he said softly before he switched to another caller. He wished he could leave right then. The urge to go to her and hold her—to protect her—overwhelmed him.

So he texted her as he was wrapping up his show.

Can I come over?

Her reply was immediate: *Yes*.

Lola was waiting for him in her doorway when he arrived. She wore monkey pajama bottoms and a tank top with pink bra straps showing. Her hair was in a haphazard bunch at the back of her head and her face was free of the war paint most women wore all the time.

She was stunning.

She held her arms open and he walked right into them.

He nestled his head in the crook of her neck, inhaling her, taking comfort in her. Then he hoisted her into his arms and took her inside straight to the bedroom.

Lowering her gently onto the bed, he covered her and pressed a soft kiss to her ready lips.

He felt her sigh, a breathy caress against his skin, and he held her closer.

"I'm happy you came," she whispered.

"So am I." He lifted his head. "I didn't know about your mom."

"How could you? I never told you."

The sadness in her eyes slayed him. "Why is that?"

"It's not exactly something you introduce into every day conversation."

"We're beyond that."

She gazed at him, her eyes wide and searching. "Are we?"

"Yes," he said definitely. He touched the corner of her mouth, where all her sadness seemed to gather. "What's your mom's name?"

"Sally." Lola sighed. "She was diagnosed with dementia shortly after my dad died. The doctors don't think the two are related, but I always wondered. My parents were the most in love couple ever."

He rolled onto his back and took her with him, so she draped over his body. "Where does she live?"

"In a home." She shook her head. "I hate that she's there, but taking care of her became too much for me alone, and they're one of the best care facilities in the country. It's why I moved to San Francisco.

We lived in Seattle before."

"So you uprooted yourself for your mom."

"No." She frowned. "Well, yes, but it wasn't like that. I wouldn't be a writer if it weren't for my mom."

"How so?"

Lola sighed. "I've never told anyone this. Not even my agent."

His chest swelled with pride. He wanted to encourage her, but he waited for her to tell him on her own time.

"I started writing because of my mom. Most dementia and Alzheimer's patients respond to photos or music, but my mom didn't respond to anything except the sound of my voice. So to help her remember, and to keep her engage in the present, I wrote the story of her courtship with my dad and read it out loud to her. A nurse overheard part of it and encouraged me to get it published."

"And the rest is history?"

"Yes." She looked him in the eye. "If it weren't for my mom and her sickness I don't think I'd have become a writer."

"That's tough," he said quietly, understanding the dilemma in what she was confessing. The guilt.

She cupped his face. "Thank you."

"For?"

"For coming over. For listening. For comforting." She inched closer. "For kissing."

He held her tighter. "I haven't done nearly enough of that."

"Well, what are you waiting for?" She nipped his lower lip with her teeth.

He recognized an invitation when he heard one, and he accepted.

Over and over again, until they were breathless and sweaty, sadness replaced by ecstasy.

Chapter Nineteen

TONIGHT WAS THE night.

Kristin looked at herself in the mirror. Little halter black dress. Big girl shoes. Dark red lips and smoky eyes.

But it was underneath that she was really decked out. She'd stopped by Romantic Notions, and Olivia had sold her lingerie that was sure to bring Rob to his knees. It propped and accentuated and tantalized.

She was ready.

She smiled at her reflection. Rob wasn't going to know what hit him. He expected her—she'd called to tell him she'd finished the project and wanted to deliver it to him. He just wouldn't expect her like this.

Wrapping a red shawl around her, she picked up her laptop case and walked out the door.

The cab she'd called arrived. Giddy with anticipation, she gave Rob's address and counted the seconds till they reached it.

She tipped the driver excessively and hopped out. Trying not to teeter on her heels, she rushed to the front door and rang the bell.

A moment later Rob opened it. He was still in some semblance of his work clothes: slacks, slightly undone shirt, but with bare feet. No tie.

Bummer.

"Hi." She smiled brightly, trying not to shiver in the chilling Laurel Heights wind.

"Come in." He let her pass, taking her laptop from her as she entered. "You look amazing."

"Thanks." Exhilaration rose in her chest, threatening to bubble out, but she kept it together.

"Are you going out tonight?" he asked, surveying her head to toe.

She was hoping to stay in. "I'm open to the possibilities," she said.

He frowned at her. She could tell something displeased him, but before she could ask, he ushered her in and to his study.

He set her laptop down on his desk. "Would you like anything to drink? Water? Wine?"

"Why don't I show you what I created first, and then we can go from there?"

Gesturing to the executive chair behind his desk, he pulled another seat close and sat down. "And then I have something I want to say. About the other night."

The night of innuendo and desire, as she'd come to think of it. "Okay," she agreed eagerly.

Kristin took the larger chair, withdrew her laptop, and booted it. "It'll just take me a sec to get online and show you the database." As she logged in and waited, she told him about the bells and whistles she'd added.

When she finished, he was staring at her like she was an alien. "That's over and beyond what I expected," he explained.

"Wait till you actually see it." She turned her laptop to him so he could inspect the beta interface. "That's a copy on my own server. I didn't want to mess with your databases until you greenlighted everything I've done."

She let him go through the site, testing out all the featuring, while she watched his face. She recognized the nuances of his expressions, so she knew the intensity behind his gaze was excitement.

At least she hoped it was.

She resisted the urge to run her foot against his leg. For good measure, she sat on her hands to keep them to herself, too.

Finally, he looked up. "This is incredible."

"I know! Did you notice the graphing functionality I added?"

"Yes, and the choices to toggle between the different types of graphs." He clicked a couple buttons. "When you said you could take care of this for me, I never expected *this*."

"I'm really quite good."

"I'm beginning to see that." He pushed the laptop away and leaned back to stare at her.

She batted her eyes. "Want me to stand up and twirl or something?"

"I'm just wondering how it is that you work in a café when you can do this." He waved at her laptop.

Some of her pleasure faded. "I like working in a café, at least for the time being."

"It seems like some of your skills are lost there."

"Maybe."

"You'd make more money in tech."

No kidding. Been there, done that. "That's definitely true."

"Some part of you has to like it, to do it so well."

"I love coding, but I'm not doing it for profit," she said resolutely.

"What was this then?"

An act of friendship, and possibly more.

"If you can make money doing this," he continued, "couldn't you do it at least on a part-time, consulting level?"

She only wanted to do it for him, to make him happy. But something held her back from saying that. She simply said, "No, I really couldn't."

"Not even if I offered you another job?"

She stilled. "Another job?"

He reached toward her. For a moment, her heart leapt, thinking he was reaching for *her*. But he opened a drawer and pulled out a checkbook and pen. She watched as he opened it, scrawled a couple lines, and tore the check out.

Handing it to her, he smiled. "For the work you did, and there's more where that came from if you'd like another project."

Reluctantly she took the check. For most people, it'd be enough to live on for six months. To her, it was heartbreak.

She swallowed her hurt so she could speak. "Are you standing by your morals?"

"Excuse me?"

"Are you holding to your credo that you don't date people who work for you?"

"Of course." His brow furrowed. "That'll never change."

She nodded, ducking her head so he wouldn't see the hurt welling in her eyes. "What about our attraction to each other? What about that morning in Grounds for Thought? What about the other night on our walk?"

He ran a hand through his hair. For the first time since she'd met him, he couldn't meet her eyes. "It was a mistake to go there."

"A mistake," she repeated flatly.

He nodded. "I shouldn't have let it go so far, especially the other night on the walk. I was out of line. I got caught up in the moment, with the pier, the moon, the company. It was—"

"Magic?" she offered sarcastically.

"Unfortunate," he said.

Unfortunate. He called one of the greatest nights she'd ever had *unfortunate*. She got up and began to

pace. "Now I know what Julia Roberts felt like."

"What?" Rob stood and took her arm, holding her still to get her to look at him. "What are you talking about?"

"Julia Roberts in *Pretty Woman,* when Richard Gere wanted to pay her off for helping him when all she wanted was a kiss."

"A kiss?"

"A kiss." She grabbed his shirt and yanked him forward to meet her mouth.

It should have been bitter and awkward. Instead it was the most perfect kiss she'd ever shared. The perfect balance of heat and moisture, passion and tenderness.

She lifted her head slowly, hovering within reach if he wanted her enough to take her. She looked into his eyes, half-lidded with desire, and then socked his chest. "How can you not see this?"

"What?" he asked, catching her hands in his.

"*This*. I'd gesture to the two of us, but you're holding my hands."

"I didn't want you to hit me again."

Her gaze narrowed. "It'd have been so satisfying though."

"Why don't you explain what this is about, and maybe we can fix it."

"This is about us. About the attraction between us. About me wanting you, so much I redid your database to show you I could be a good partner."

He frowned. "In business?"

"In life," she shouted. "Give me my hands back."

The instant he let go of her she hopped up and began gathering her things. "I was so stupid. It's my ovaries' fault."

"I'm not sure I understand that."

"No kidding." She glared at him. "You wouldn't understand a meteor if it fell right on top of you."

"I hesitate to ask this, but does that make sense?"

She faced him and growled.

"Explain your ovaries to me," he said in a beast-taming voice.

"The second my ovaries saw you they went *insane. Pick him, pick him,*" she said in a sing-song, mocking voice, waving her arms. "But it wasn't just that I was foolish enough to think you'd make a good sperm donor. I genuinely *liked* you. I thought maybe you liked me too. So I was most stupid to start imagining actually being with you."

He stared at her.

"That's *it*?" She dropped her laptop bag on the desk and turned to him, hands on her hips. "That's all you've got for me? That implacable stare that says so little and so much at the same time?"

"You've taken me by surprise," he said.

"Then you're *especially* an idiot, because I've all but thrown myself at you. And you wanted me throwing myself at you! Or maybe that's where I was the idiot, in thinking you wanted me. Only the joke's on me, right? Because I was wooing you, but you were offering me a job." Shaking her head, she grabbed her bag and started to leave. "I don't need you to take care of me. I need you to be a partner who sees me as an equal, who wants to build and share a family with me."

"Shouldn't you think about cleaning up your life first?" he asked, following after her. "Then we can discuss a future together."

She whirled and faced him. "My life is plenty clean, and that's bullshit. According to you, you won't date anyone you employ, so how can I believe you're going to make an exception for me? You know what I think?"

"What?" he asked cautiously.

"You're ashamed of me." She held her hand up to stop him from speaking. "You like me. You're obviously turned on by me. So whatever hesitation you have must be my job. You don't want to date a barista."

"That's not true." He frowned at her, stepping closer. "I just want you to turn your life around first. Then we can talk about the future."

"The future is now!" she yelled. "I don't have time for the future to be later. My ovaries are shriveling more by the day. I want children, and I want them with you."

To prove her point, she grabbed him and kissed him one more time—in case he missed it all the other times.

When she released him, they were both panting hard. Voice low, she looked him in the eye and said, "You can't tell me you don't feel that. You can't tell me your heart doesn't want me, that you don't look forward to seeing me, and that you don't miss my face when it's not around."

He was quiet, but then he said, "Is that enough?"

Growling, she flounced away, walking to the front door. Hurt. "Would it be enough if I was a

white-collar worker? If I wore heels and power suits and went in to a cubicle every day? If I sat in gray walls and was miserable? Because you're saying that it might be."

"I—"

"I used to do that," she yelled over whatever he was going to say. "I used to rule the world. Ever heard of Aspire? Well, that used to be my baby before I realized that I wanted a living, breathing one instead of who'd give something back to me beyond just more zeros in my bank account."

"Aspire, the consulting firm?"

"Are you impressed now?" She reached the front door and opened it.

"Where are you going?" he asked, coming up behind her.

"I'm taking my eggs and going away to find someone who appreciates me for more than my money-making ability."

"That's not what I was saying," he called after her.

"Then I must not understand English," she said over her shoulder. She rushed to the street and then blindly turned in a direction, not caring where she was going as long as it was away.

Chapter Twenty

"LOUISE IS IN love with Sawyer," her mom declared after Lola finished reading the selection she'd brought.

Startled by the decree, Lola looked up from her purse, where she was tucking away the pages. "How do you know?"

"It's obvious," her mom said simply as she knitted.

Lola sat and watched her mom's nimble fingers. Was her mom right? Was she in love with Sam?

She'd always expected love to be a thunderbolt—a big blast that rocked the center of her universe. With Sam it'd started as an irritation, a reluctant attraction, and grown into something warm and fuzzy that made her grin like a loon when she thought of it.

Was that love?

It felt like it, especially if the effervescent giddiness inside her as she thought about him was any indication.

How did Sam feel?

He liked her—that she knew without a doubt. And he trusted her, otherwise he wouldn't have let her anywhere around his daughter.

She shook her head. She was playing tit-for-tat with the emotion, waiting to decide if she loved him based on whether he loved her. Love didn't work that way. Love happened, whether you wanted it to or not. Whether the other person reciprocated or not.

Her problem was that she was afraid to trust someone after what had happened with Kevin. If she were writing herself as a heroine, she'd make the character realize that sometimes in life you got burned. That was the essence of living. You couldn't very well hide from life, right?

Well—you *could*. But where would the fun be?

"I think I might take a nap," her mom said, setting down her knitting. Then she looked around the room, her face paling in alarm. "Why aren't I in my room? Where am I?"

Lola got up quickly to keep her mother from panicking. "You're in your room, Mom."

"No, I'm not." Her voice rose and she tried to rush to her feet. "My room has green paint on the walls."

Lola tried to keep her voice as even and calm as she could. "Your old room had green paint, but you don't live in that house anymore."

Sally blinked, then her face went blank and she stopped struggling.

Lola pushed aside the futile anger and grief and helped her mother shuffle into bed. She almost wished her mom were still in her delusion instead of catatonic. She went to kiss her mom's forehead, but Sally had already turned around and was sound asleep.

She sat on the edge of the bed, touching her mom's back. Feeling her warm back made her feel like her mom was the same as she'd always been when Lola was a kid and used to climb into bed with her.

But it was a fairy tale.

Gathering her things, she left, feeling heavy. She should have gone home and gotten back to work, but her heart wasn't in it, so she stopped at Grounds for Thought instead.

Eve was manning the counter, looking radiant

and happy. Eve was one of those perpetually polished women who couldn't look disheveled if she tried. Lola imagined that if she worked in a kitchen all day, she'd be splattered and shiny. Eve always looked like she'd stepped out of an Ann Taylor catalog.

She was talking a woman at the counter who looked like an angel from an Italian master's painting. Aqualine nose and long, curly brown hair. Lola stared at the woman, seeing a story behind the sad almond-shaped eyes and wondering what it was.

"Hi, Lola," Eve called out when she saw her. "Come meet Daniela."

The woman turned to her and gave her a smile that didn't quite reach her eyes. "Nice to meet you."

Somehow, Lola knew Daniela's lack of warmth had nothing to do with her. In fact, she could relate, because she wasn't in the perkiest mood herself.

"Daniela's moving into the neighborhood. She's a dessert *artiste*. She's making the cake for my wedding."

"Oh, right." Lola nodded, remembering. "You wrote a cookbook."

"It was the hardest thing I've ever done," the woman admitted. "Harder than culinary academy even."

"Tell me about it, but not really, because I already know." She grinned.

"Lola writes romance novels," Eve explained.

Daniela blinked once, and then it was like her whole being came to life. "Lola Carmichael?"

"Yes."

"I've read your books. You're a great writer," Daniela effused. "I just read your latest book on the flight out from New York. I finished it and started reading it again immediately."

"You're either sweet or crazy," Lola said with a teasing smile.

"I like to think I'm sweet, but my assistant might debate that." She stood up and faced Eve. "Thanks for the information, Eve."

"Treat's expecting your call. He's the best contractor out there, and I don't say that because he's my fiancé." She smiled like a woman in love. "He can get your remodeling back on track."

The chef sighed. "I'll call him. It was nice meeting you, Lola. I hope you stop by when I get my storefront open and say hi."

They watched her stride out of there.

"She seems unhappy," Lola ventured.

"She does. I discreetly offered to listen, but she doesn't know me well enough to trust me yet." Eve frowned at her. "Do you trust me enough to tell me what's wrong?"

Lola blinked at the café owner. Then she surprised herself by saying, "I'm in love."

Eve grinned. "Congratulations."

"He doesn't know." She pursed her lips. "It may be more accurate to state that he may not reciprocate."

"Ah. I have just the thing."

Lola watched Eve begin a seemingly complicated drink that involved stirring, steaming, and stirring some more. A flourish, and it was in a cup being pushed toward her.

She took a sip. Hot chocolate, only it was so much more. Silky and dark, with just enough sweet to balance the bitter.

"Delicious," she said, trying not to gulp the hot liquid down. "A shot of vodka and it'd be perfect."

"No wonder you and Gwen are friends." Chuckling, Eve looked up as the door chimed someone's entrance. "Excuse me a second."

Lola nodded, hands cupped around her drink,

thinking about Sam. It seemed like forever since she'd seen him—he'd had Madison the past couple days. She missed him—a lot.

She'd go home and call him, she decided. The idea of talking to him was strangely comforting. She wondered if she could discuss her feelings about him *with* him. She had a feeling she could. She trusted him.

"Lola!"

She looked up to find Madison rushing over to her. Grinning she stood up to give the girl a hug.

Sam must be there. Lola's heart leapt in pleasure, and she realized that maybe talking out her feelings wasn't necessary. Maybe she'd already fallen.

Searching behind Madison for Sam, she only saw an aggressively thin, coldly beautiful brunette with calculating eyes.

Sam's ex-wife. Lola knew it without a doubt.

As if she suddenly remembered she was with her mom, Madison stopped short, her eyes wide as she obviously decided it wasn't a good idea to hug her dad's girlfriend in front of her mom.

Lola smiled reassuringly. "How's it going, Madison? You're far from home."

"We were close by, and Grounds for Thought has the best hot chocolate ever." She glanced at her mom, obviously not sure what to do.

Not wanting the girl to be punished for anything, Lola turned to the other woman. "I'm Lola, a friend of Sam's. You must be Madison's mom. It's Chelsea, right?"

"Yes," the woman said coolly. She didn't offer a hand or even the remnants of a smile. She just stared, part curious and part hostile.

Lola could see her in Madison, but Madison had enough of her father to balance out the sharpness. This woman was all edge. She must have made Sam's life hell.

Just when she thought Chelsea was just going to give her the silent treatment, she said, "Madison, why don't you go order your drink while I talk to Lola."

Madison glanced between the two of them, worry creasing her forehead. Lola nodded reassuringly at her and then returned her attention to Sam's ex.

"You've been spending a lot of time with my daughter," Chelsea said once Madison had moved away.

Not that the girl couldn't hear them. She wanted to point out that the register was a mere four feet

from where they stood. But she just said, "Madison's wonderful. You must be proud of her."

"Fortunately, she takes after me." *Rather than her father* was implied.

"You and Sam have done a lovely job raising her."

Chelsea must have heard the sincerity in her voice because she frowned. "You care about him. You poor, poor thing."

"Um..."

"It's such a shame you've fallen for Sam's lies." She tsked, shaking her head.

Lies? Lola blinked. Maybe she'd entered the Twilight Zone?

"Sam *is* very convincing, so you can't take all the blame yourself."

Blame? She shook her head. "Convincing about what?"

"About his affections." Chelsea's eyes widened. "Don't worry, sweetie, you aren't the first woman to fall for lines, and you won't be the last."

She wanted to disagree—Sam was genuine with her. But as she started to argue in his favor, she remembered his program manager Jennifer and the brokenhearted way she looked at Sam.

No, Sam like her—Lola knew that without a doubt. No one could fake the tenderness and excitement he showed when he was with her. Why would he?

His ex-wife, on the other hand, had every reason to try to sabotage his relationships. He'd described her as bitchy, and she was living up to that assessment.

Lola wouldn't fall for the woman's bait. She wasn't that gullible.

Chelsea continued blithely. "Granted, I believe he actually does care, at least until he gets bored and moves on."

"He didn't seem that type."

"I think I'm more qualified than you to describe his type," the woman said dryly. She shrugged. "Believe what you will."

Madison rejoined them, a hot chocolate in one hand and a little bag in the other, her gaze darting between the two of them. "Mom?"

"Let's go, Madison." The woman pivoted on her heels and strode out.

Madison shot Lola an apologetic wince. "Sorry."

"There's nothing to be sorry about." Lola smiled

at her, running her hand on the girl's hair. "Go catch up. Maybe I'll see you this weekend."

She lit up. "Okay!" she exclaimed, hurrying after her mom.

What had she gotten herself into, dating a man with baggage like this? Lola shook her head.

At the door, Madison turned around and gave her a wide grin before running outside after her mom.

Lola's heart turned over. Okay, maybe it was worth it. Then she thought about Sam—his kisses, how he respected her work, and then way he touched her, like she was sacred.

It was definitely worth it.

Chapter Twenty-one

FOR SOMETHING DIFFERENT to do, Sam had suggested going to a jazz club on Fillmore. Happy to be taken out, Lola had told Sam she'd meet him at the radio station for their date.

Before she left, she checked her official author email to see if anything needed her attention. There was a bunch of fan mail, some spam, some marketing emails, another email from Kevin asking for his T-shirt back, and one from a couple days before entitled *TOP SECRET—Very, Very Important!* from Madison Taylor.

Curious, she opened it.

To: Lola Carmichael <lola@lolacarmichael.com>

From: Madison Taylor <mad_tee@hotmail.com>

Subject: TOP SECRET—Very, Very Important!

Hi Lola! Sorry to bother you, but I have a problem and I need to tell someone, but I can't tell my mom or dad. But you HAVE to keep it TOP SECRET. Okay?

Today I fell in love for the first time ever. His name is Jeff, and he's twelve years old.

I just wanted to tell someone. But you can't tell Daddy. Or my mom. They'll kill me.

Madison

Utterly charmed, Lola archived the email. One day ten, fifteen years from now, she'd show Madison that email and they'd share a secret smile.

Assuming she was with Sam still.

Hope rose inside her, and she touched her chest where it all gathered. Maybe. Definitely maybe.

But one thing was certain: no way was she telling Sam. He'd go ballistic if he thought a boy was sniff-ing around his little girl. Watching him navigate that minefield when Madison started dating was going to be entertaining.

She arrived at the station right as his show ended. She poked her head into his sound booth, per his instructions.

He grinned when he saw her, but continued to speak into the microphone. "Next week we've got an exciting lineup, including Jonas James, past life regressionist and relationship psychic. This is Sam Taylor, and thank you for joining us at *Ladies' Night*."

He cued the cheesy music and took off his headphones. "I hate the theme music."

"It's sappy." She walked toward him.

"I think they got John Tesh to record it." He stood up and slipped his arms her. "Hi."

"Hi."

He lowered his mouth to hers and greeted her properly. He was smiling when he lifted his head. "Hi," he said again.

She laughed. "Are we going? This girl's had a long day and could use a cocktail, jazz, and some canoodling time with her man."

"I don't think I've ever canoodled before, but I'm always willing to try something new." He kissed her quickly. "I've just got one thing to take care of. Wait here and I'll be right back."

"Okay." She watched him leave and then sat in his chair. It was still warm from his body, and she thought she could almost smell his yummy scent.

The door opened. She sat up, thinking it was Sam, but it was his program manager, Jennifer.

The woman looked more startled than Lola felt. "Lola?"

She smiled her welcome. "It's nice to see you again."

"Are you here for Sam?"

There was an overtly incredulous tone to her words. Lola frowned. Why was that so unbelievable? "He should be right back, if you're looking for him."

Jennifer shook her head. "I almost can't believe you're here."

"Why not?"

"I didn't think it'd last. Sam goes through women so quickly."

Not this again. Lola stifled a groan. Had anyone even considered that maybe he went through so many women just because he hadn't met the right one?

"I thought he liked you," Jennifer continued, "but I wasn't sure it'd last. He has commitment issues. Then, at first, I suspected he was faking it to get his job back, but now I see he's sincere in it."

"His job back?" she repeated, frowning.

"The sports show." Jennifer's eyes widened as though she just realized she'd stepped in something vile. "I don't know what I was saying. Forget it."

"Why would he have to fake being with me to get his job back?" Lola persisted.

"No reason." The woman looked at her naked wrist. "Look at the time! Gotta go."

Lola was still sitting there, perplexed, not sure what to think, when Sam came back. "Okay, I'm ready. Let's go."

His smile looked genuine. He looked happy to see her—delighted even.

Was he faking it after all?

She'd given him the benefit of doubt after Chelsea's ambush. Of course, she had. Who was she going to believe: him or his bitter ex-wife? But Jennifer's accidental confession backed up what Chelsea had said.

Lola studied him. Was she being blind to his faults? Delusional? Building castles where there wasn't even a real foundation?

Call her crazy, but she still had faith in Sam.

Then what was that about getting his job back?

His sports program? She knew he'd somehow been demoted into *Ladies' Night* and that Jennifer had been somehow responsible for it.

His smile faded into concern. "Are you okay, Lola? You look pale."

"I'm fine," she lied. She stood up and tried to smile but failed, because all she could hear was Jennifer saying *I suspected he was faking it to get his job back.*

What did that mean? What was he hiding? And why was he hiding it from her?

Something was wrong with Lola.

He watched her as she watched the jazz quartet. She'd barely touched her drink, and though she appeared to be listening, she felt a million miles away. She wasn't even holding his hand—she'd maneuvered herself so it wasn't possible.

She'd greeted him like normal, but when he'd returned she'd been weird. Something must have happened in that interim period.

But what?

"Lola," he finally said, leaning toward her.

She looked at him with what was supposed to

be a smile, but she just looked like she was going to puke. "Yes?" she asked politely.

"Come on." He took her hand and dragged her away from the table.

Scrambling to get her purse and coat, she hissed. "What are you doing?"

"Getting to the bottom of things." He took her outside and down a couple buildings before turning her to face him. "Tell me what's wrong."

She looked like she was going to debate that anything was the matter. Then she lifted her chin and looked him defiantly in the eyes. "I talked to Jennifer tonight."

His punishment.

He didn't have to ask anything more—he saw that was precisely it.

Damn it.

Exhaling, he said, "Jennifer wanted to teach me a lesson—"

"For breaking her heart." Lola nodded.

"For hurting her unwittingly. She wanted to teach me a lesson in love, so she yanked me from my sports talk program and put me on *Ladies' Night*." He shook his head. "That's it."

"Why would you fake being with me?"

Jesus H, Jennifer. He was going to strangle her. "The deal was, if I could sustain a relationship for a period of time, Jennifer would give me my old show back. But it turns out I'm good with the lovelorn. My standings kick ass. I'm considering doing a love show once a week even after I return to sports talk."

"If it was such a non-issue, why did you hide the deal from me?"

He couldn't answer that. He searched for something plausible, but he couldn't come up with anything. Because he was in the wrong here. "I'm sorry, Lola. I should have told you."

"Yes, you should have. Because you know what this looks like?" She poked a finger at his chest. "That you used me to get your old job back."

"No one's that good an actor."

"I thought the same, but what's there to act about? The sex is good and I'm convenient. It's win-win for you."

He took her by the arms. "It wasn't like that."

"I wouldn't have thought so, only you didn't tell me. So what am I supposed to think except that there was something to hide?"

"Lola—"

"Tell me that at no time did it cross your mind that I was the answer to your problems," she demanded.

Sam winced.

"That was the loudest answer you could have given." She detached herself from him and began to walk away.

"Lola, wait." He kept pace alongside her. "I admit, it may have crossed my mind, but that's not why I'm with you."

"Excuse me for being skeptical." She kept her gaze forward, not looking at him. "Especially after what both Jennifer and Chelsea said."

"*Chelsea*? My ex-wife Chelsea?"

"How many Chelseas do you know?" she asked scathingly.

Good point. "When did you meet her?"

"She and Madison stopped by Grounds for Thought while I happened to be there."

Great—he could just imagine how that meeting went. "And you talked to her?"

"She didn't leave me any choice."

"That sounds like her." He took Lola's hand. "I'm sorry."

"Why?" She stopped abruptly, facing him. "Because she blew your cover by telling me how you toss women aside once you've got them? You know, I didn't believe her because she's your ex, but Jennifer said the same thing, and Jennifer is a nice person. So what am I supposed to think?"

He tugged her closer. "Believe that I love you."

"Do you? Or are you just saying it because I'm a means to an end?" She disengaged from him and began walking again. "You screwed up. You had a future here. Love and fun and support."

"Had?" For the first time, real worry gripped his heart.

She glanced at him. "You had the team you've been missing all these years."

"Just like that, you're going to leave? You're going to give up?" he asked, angry.

"I'd be foolish to hang around and trust my heart to you, right?" She stepped onto the street and waved for a passing cab.

The cab stopped, and he helplessly watched her get inside. It felt just like his ski accident, where he witnessed the whole thing in slow motion but was powerless to stop it. And just like that day, he felt like life was crashing down on him, except this time it was completely his own fault.

Chapter Twenty-two

LOLA SLUMPED ON a stool next to Gwen's worktable, watching her friend sketch a new design. Not her hands—Lola watched her face as she drew.

The first thing she'd noticed about Gwen the day they'd met was the light in her eyes. Gwen's spirit shined through. Now that Gwen was in a relationship, that indefinable quality was magnified. Gwen simply glowed.

"If I didn't love you, I'd hate you," Lola said listlessly.

Her friend set her sketchpad down with a slap. "That's it. You've been moping around here too long. Get up."

"Are you kicking me out?"

"No, I'm taking you for a treat."

Lola momentarily perked up. "Hot chocolate at Eve's?"

"Whatever you want." Gwen slipped her shoes back on and grabbed a jacket. "As long as you either talk about what's bothering you or stop wallowing in it."

"Those are my only two options?"

"Yes."

She sighed.

"Well?" Gwen asked as they walked out of the store.

"I'm weighing my options."

"Come on." Gwen linked an arm through hers. "We'll get you hot chocolate—"

"And a chocolate chip cookie."

Gwen rolled her eyes. "Hot chocolate *and* a chocolate chip cookie, and then you have to tell me what's going on, although I suspect this has to do with a man."

"Men suck."

"They do, don't they?" To her credit, Gwen tried not to smile.

Lola made a face at her. "I didn't mock you in your time of need."

"No, you're a good friend." They walked into Grounds for Thought and went to sit at the empty seats at the bar.

Eve's most recent hire, Kristin, came over to them and leaned on the counter. "What can I get you ladies?"

"My friend here"—Gwen pointed at her—"will have a hot chocolate and chocolate chip cookie. I'd like a chai, please."

Kristin looked at Lola knowingly. "A heartbreak special?"

"Is it that obvious?"

The barista shrugged as she started to steam milk. "I've been pounding down the hot chocolates myself. Men suck."

Lola poked Gwen. "*See?*"

Gwen just shook her head. "Men don't suck, they're misunderstood, and sometimes they're idiots. But you can't quit them each time they do stupid things. You'll be alone forever, and what fun would that be?"

The door opened and a man walked in.

Actually, he *stalked,* Lola decided. It didn't help that he had shaggy hair and was built like the hulk—the Eric Bana hulk, not the Bill Bixby one. His gaze darted to every corner, as though casing the joint or checking for assassins.

He headed directly to the counter and stared at Kristin.

The barista pointed at him. "Don't act cute. I'm not in the mood."

"Cute?" he said, his voice low and growly.

"Don't deny that's what you were going for. But I'm telling you now, you're not my type." She handed him a cup of coffee and waved. "It's on me today."

He narrowed his eyes suspiciously. "Why?"

Kristin's gaze narrowed, too, and she leaned toward him across the counter. "Are you challenging me?"

He studied her like she was a foreign creature he'd never encountered. Then he shook his head and walked out.

Gwen exhaled the moment the front door closed behind him. "I thought he was going to eat you up."

"I'd let him," the barista said, sliding their beverages toward them. "He looks like he's got strong sperm."

Lola choked on her cocoa. Gwen just gawked.

"Just an observation." Kristin shrugged. "I meant it when I said he wasn't my type. I seem to go for aloof rather than surly."

"Excuse me?"

All three of them turned to the voice. It belonged to a redhead with pale skin. She was dressed fashionably but professionally in a dress with a little sweater over it. But she was so thin Lola had the urge to feed her peanut butter sandwiches.

The young woman's confident smile was undermined by the hesitation in her eyes. But, to her credit, she forged ahead. "I couldn't help but overhear your conversation about men, and I thought I could help."

"Are you a hitman?" Kristin asked.

The woman blushed. "No. I'm a matchmaker."

Gwen perked up. "Really?"

She nodded as she handed each of them a card.

Lola had expected it to be covered in hearts, but instead it was tastefully abstract but feminine. On the back, it read:

Valentine Jones
Matchmaker
www.ValentineMatch.com
415.555.3597

"Yes, my name is really Valentine," the woman said before any of them could say a word.

Hearing the resignation in her voice, Lola patted

her arm in sympathy. "Sometimes parents just don't realize what they're doing."

Gwen flipped the card over. "Your office is just a couple blocks away."

"I just opened it." Valentine smiled proudly. "Off Sacramento, on Walnut."

"Welcome to the neighborhood," Gwen said.

"Anyway, I can find a great guy for you." She looked at them hopefully. "I'm offering a discount, too."

"Well, I'll definitely keep it in mind." Kristin tucked the card into her bra. "Once I get over being bitter about Rob."

"Who's Rob?" Lola asked.

"A loser." Although the way she said it showed she didn't actually believe that.

"Well." Valentine cleared her throat. "I'll get on my way. I hope you guys stop by."

"She was cute," Gwen said after the woman left. Then she turned to Lola. "So we know Kristin's bitter about a loser. What's your story?"

She sighed. "I'm bitter too. The man I was dating was using me."

"For sex?" the barista asked as she wiped the

counter. "Because that wouldn't be so bad under certain circumstances."

"To get his job back." Lola frowned. "The thing is, I'm mostly angry at myself."

"For trusting him?" Gwen offered.

"No, because when I realized I was in love with him I decided it didn't matter how he felt about me, because my feelings were real, and even if he didn't love me it was a gift to have those feelings again. And then I go and get pissed at him, when really he hadn't made any promises to me. He just made me feel special, and shouldn't that be a good thing?"

Gwen frowned. "Well—"

"But then I *am* angry," she continued, smacking her fist on the counter. "If he hadn't meant to lose me, why didn't he just tell me his job was on the line unless he dated someone steadily for a period of time? He lied to me."

"Bastard," Kristin said.

"But he's not." Lola wilted. "He's really a nice guy, underneath the swagger and the baggage. He's called me every night since the fight."

"What did he say?"

"I don't know. I haven't taken his calls."

"Lola." Gwen shook her head.

No way was she going to admit he'd left her a note, too, in case she hadn't been getting his messages. It'd been a sweet note, too, asking her to just hear him out.

But she was scared. She didn't trust herself with him. Was she creating the relationship she wanted out of fairy dust, or was Sam for real? And how could she tell?

"Lola." Gwen leaned toward her. "What does your heart want?"

Her heart wanted him.

But it'd also wanted Kevin.

Was she going to let it lead her astray again? How did she trust it?

Chapter Twenty-three

NOT EVEN WATCHING *Dirty Dancing* helped.

Lola slouched on her couch, watching Patrick Swayze lift Jennifer Grey for the millionth time, knowing she should be writing the end to her story. The problem was she had no idea how the story ended.

She looked at the whiteboard on the wall, where she'd brainstormed out possible endings.

Louise meets Gerard Butler and forgets about Sawyer.

Louise moves to a small hippie town, stops shaving her legs, and spends the rest of her life making voodoo dolls for women who've been scorned.

Louise doesn't answer Sawyer's calls, buys three cats, and lives alone for all eternity in her cold apartment.

And, finally:

Louise forgives him, asks for forgiveness herself, and they live happily ever after.

That ending seemed especially farfetched.

Her phone rang. She debated not answering it, but then in the end she picked it up. "Heartbreak Hotel, proprietor and sole resident speaking."

There was a chuckle. "It's Eve, Lola."

"Oh. Hi."

"You have a visitor waiting for you at my café."

"A visitor?" *Sam*? She shot up, her heart racing.

"She's cute, but she was very effusive about my hot chocolate so I was predisposed to think that."

"Madison." Lola hauled herself up and scrounged under the couch for her flip-flops. "What's she doing there?"

"Waiting for you. I take it you didn't realize she was coming to see you?"

"No. Is she with anyone?"

"She's alone."

Stranger and stranger. "Keep her safe. I'll be there in two minutes."

She hung up, redid her ponytail so she looked less

insane, grabbed a hoodie, and hurried to Grounds for Thought.

Madison sat on a stool at the counter, nibbling on a Madeleine. She lit up the moment she saw Lola.

"Hey," Lola said, grabbing the seat next to the kid and moving it closer. "This is a surprise."

"A bad surprise?" the girl asked hesitantly.

"I love seeing you so, no, it'd never be a bad surprise." Lola brushed the hair out of Madison's eyes. "But how'd you get here?"

"The bus."

"Alone?"

She nodded. "But I ride the bus alone all the time."

"Do your mom and dad know where you are?"

Madison shrank in on herself. "Not really."

"Oh, Madison." Pulling out her phone, Lola shot Sam a quick text: *Madison is with me. She's fine. I'll get her home safely.*

Then she put her phone away and faced the girl. "It's not cool to take off without anyone knowing where you are. If something happens, it helps if people know where you were headed. So don't do this again."

"Okay." Madison grimaced. "Are you really mad at me?"

"I'm not mad at all. I just don't want you to be hurt." She hugged the girl, who clenched her tight. Running a hand down her hair, Lola closed her eyes against the swelling of her heart. Apparently, she'd fallen in love with the daughter as well as the father.

Damn it.

Madison looked up at her. "Did I do something to mess things up with you and Daddy?"

"Of course not." Lola scowled. "Why do you think that?"

The girl shrugged, looking miserable. "I thought maybe because I brought my mom here. Maybe you didn't like her."

She hadn't really, but Madison didn't need to know that. "It has nothing to do with you or your mom, and everything to do with me and your dad."

"Daddy is really sad."

Lola narrowed her eyes. "Are you sure he didn't send you here?"

"No way." She shook her head vigorously. "He's going to kill me when I go home. Then he'll ground me till I'm forty."

"Knowing this, you still came?"

"Well, yeah." She looked at Lola like Lola was smoking crack. "Daddy met you and he was happy again, like he used to be when I was a kid. Now he's all moping and sad again."

How coincidental—*she* was moping and sad too.

"He likes you a lot." Madison looked at her with a child's candor. "I really like you too, and I hated all the other girls my dad dated. So if it's my fault you left, I'm sorry."

"It's not your fault. Your dad and I are just being"—stupid, really—"adults."

Madison frowned. "Since you're adults for life, does that mean you won't be together anymore?"

Lola sighed. "I don't know what it means."

"Don't you like him?"

"I like him a lot."

"Is what he did that bad then?" the girl asked hesitantly.

"Your dad is a great guy," she said unequivocally. "He'd never do anything bad, but he did do something that hurt me."

Madison nodded. "Everyone makes mistakes."

And she wasn't exempt either, because she hadn't

given him a chance to apologize or make it up to her. She swallowed thickly. "Is he really miserable?"

Madison turned puppy dog eyes on her. "Not even I can cheer him up."

Lola nodded, feeling a little lighter. Not that she was happy that he felt wretched—okay, she was just the teensiest bit—but because maybe he really did like her. And people did make mistakes.

Maybe her heart *had* been trustworthy.

She took one of Madison's cookies and nibbled on it. "How's *your* love life coming along?"

The girl sighed and then swigged her hot chocolate. "Love sucks."

Lola slung an arm around Madison's shoulders. "Welcome to the club, kid."

Lola sat in her agent's office, staring out the window. Instead of the sun peeking from the clouds, all she saw was the expression of longing on Sam's face when she dropped Madison off at his apartment.

She missed that face.

Sighing, she turned her attention to Paul, who was flipping through her manuscript. She should

have been more concerned about his reaction but she knew this was a good book. Her editor would love it and her fans would go crazy over it.

Paul got to the end, stared at the last page, and then looked at her. "There's no ending."

"You're so observant."

"Need I remind you that your publisher is paying for a beginning, middle, and an end?"

"I understand that." She sat up. "I just don't how it works out."

"Figure it out. You don't have much time." He pushed the manuscript across his desk at her.

She took it and put it in her purse. Next stop: her mom. She stood up and murmured a goodbye.

As she exited the office, Paul called out, "Lola."

She looked over her shoulder.

He pointed at her bag. "That's the best thing you've ever written."

Nodding, she kept walking. She'd realized Louise and Sawyer were good—in fiction. In real life, she and Sam were...

Combustible.

Comfortable.

Confounding.

She shook her head as she hailed a cab.

Still contemplating the situation, when she arrived at The Sunrise Care Home, she walked automatically up the stairs to her mom's floor.

"Lola, wait."

Startling out of her thoughts, she turned to find Letty leaning out of the nurses' station. Lola smiled faintly. "Sorry, Letty. I was lost in my head. How are you?"

"I'm good." Her tone implied someone else wasn't, and her somber look didn't help any.

The polite smile faded from Lola's lips. "My mom?"

"Yes."

Worry made her stomach jump. "I'm not going to like whatever you're going to say, am I?"

"I'm afraid not." Letty sighed. "The congestion in Sally's chest has built up again and has been resistant to medication. The doctor put her on heavy antibiotics this time."

"Okay." She nodded. "It's not something to worry too much about, right?"

Letty paused. "We just want to be careful with her."

"That's not reassuring."

The nurse patted her arm. "Seeing you will help her. She's always so happy after you're here."

Not that her mom knew who she was, she thought sadly. Lola straightened her shoulders. But her story was sure to lift her mom's spirits.

Instead of knitting, her mom was lying in bed. At first, Lola thought she was asleep, but then she saw her eyes flutter.

"Hi, Mom." She carefully sat on the edge of the bed, not wanting to freak her out. "It's me. Lola."

It was always unpredictable how her mother would react, but there was always a reaction, even if it was being freaked out for a moment before she settled back into the cloudy haze of her dementia. Today she didn't even stir.

Lola touched her mother's forehead. "Mom?" she said softly. "How are you feeling?"

Still no response.

She sat there, unsure about what to do and scared. Shifting to face her mom, she accidentally kicked her purse over.

The story.

Taking it out, she said in a chipper voice, "You

ready for your chapters today, Mom? We're getting to the part where Louise and Sawyer fall in love."

Sally stirred.

Heartened, Lola began reading the latest chapters, all the way to the black moment when Louise and Sawyer were seemingly finished forever. And then she stopped, because that was all she'd written.

Her mom lifted her head. "Louise made a mistake," she said in a weak, raspy voice.

"You think so, Mom?"

Her mom hummed. "She should have trusted him a little. But he should have been honest with her, too. It's okay. They'll find their way together."

There was a pause, and then her mom added, "Louise is a good girl. She deserves to be happy."

Tears clouded Lola's vision, and she blinked quickly. "Sometimes she doubts if she'll ever find her Happily Ever After."

"Then she should have more faith, in love and in herself." Turning over, Sally snuggled into a ball and feel asleep, her breathing labored.

Lola sat there next to her mom for a while, letting her tears fall. Her mom was right—she deserved a Happily Ever After, and she wanted it with Sam.

Did he want one with her?

She didn't know, and she'd never know as long as she was sulking. She had to ask him. She shared half the responsibility in their relationship—and complete responsibility for herself.

Wiping her cheeks, she kissed her mom. "I love you, Mom. I'm going to find my Happily Ever After."

First things first. As soon as she was outside, she pulled out her phone and dialed a number she never thought she'd call again.

His voicemail picked up. "You've reached Kevin. I can't take your call right now, but..."

She tuned out the rest of his long-winded message, waiting impatiently for her cue to speak. Finally, the tone sounded and she said, "It's Lola. I'm mailing your T-shirt back to you. Have a good life."

That done, she deleted his number from her phone and flagged a taxi. There was just one more thing left to do. She needed to write her happy ending.

Chapter Twenty-four

UNABLE TO SLEEP, Kristin went for a vigorous walk. Not where she'd walked with Rob—she wasn't a masochist—but a brisk trek up and down the hills of her neighborhood, hoping she'd exhaust herself into slumber.

It was a vain hope.

And the walk reminded her of Rob anyway. She missed him, which was crazy because she'd never had him.

"Stupid," she muttered at herself, huddling in her sweatshirt. She should have kept her eye on the ball and just asked him to have sex with her a couple times. By thinking they could have more, she'd lost out on everything.

The sad thing: she was more upset about losing Rob than she was about not having a baby. Only she hadn't lost Rob, because her relationship with Rob had been only in her head.

The sadder thing: if she'd had to choose between Rob and a baby, she'd have picked him.

She wrapped her arms around her waist and apologized to her potential child. Obviously, her hormones had gotten the best of her, and she was going crazy. What other excuse did she have for picking a random man to father her baby and then falling in love with him instead?

Because that was the craziest part of the whole situation: she'd fallen in love with Robert Cray.

"Stupid, stupid, *stupid*," she cursed herself as she marched back uphill toward her flat. She barely knew the man.

Except she did know him. She knew that he worked hard and was responsible. She knew he had a big enough heart to take in a stray mutt and hire someone to give her a hand up in the world. She knew he liked her. She knew he kissed like the world was ending, and that when he focused on a woman, for that moment she was the sum total of his world.

She wished she could have been that woman forever.

As she neared her place, she realized there was something blocking the gate.

Not something—some*one*. She squinted, trying to see in the darkness. She really needed to have a porch light installed.

Then she realized it was Rob. He sat on the top step of the path, in front of the gate, hands steepled in front of him. He was dressed more casually than she'd ever seen him, in a windbreaker and jeans. Chanel sat primly at his feet.

She stopped in place, startled out of motion. Swallowing the resurgence of regret and sudden hope, she slowly went up the walkway and stopped in front of him.

He stood as she approached. "I haven't seen you at the café in a while."

Not what she expected, but she went along with it. "I've been working in the afternoons."

"Because of me?" he asked solemnly.

Of course, because of him. But she snorted. "Don't flatter yourself."

Chanel barked once.

She reached down to pat the dog's back. God, she'd even missed the mutt.

Rob studied her. Then he surprised her by saying, "You couldn't sleep, either?"

"I was just getting exercise," she lied as she straightened. He didn't need to know how crazy she was, mooning over a man who'd never promised her anything beyond a paycheck. "What are you doing here?"

"We didn't finish our conversation. You ran out on me."

"It took you this long to act on it?"

"It took me this long to get over feeling like I'd been played for a fool."

She pretended not to understand what he was saying. "Don't blame this on me. I removed myself from a situation that was harmful to me."

"I'm harmful?" he asked with a frown.

To her heart, he was. "The potential is definitely there."

"You're the one who lied."

"*What*?"

He nodded. "You misrepresented yourself to me. I thought you were a starving woman, down on her luck. Why do you think I wanted to give you work?"

"I know you want me to think you have a bleeding heart, and the destitute woman appreciates your kindness, but she didn't need it." She crossed her

arms to keep from throwing them around him and begging him to be hers.

"*You* led me to believe you were destitute. I don't think you can fault me for wanting to see your situation improved." He stepped right up to her. "I care about you. I wanted to be your knight-in-shining-armor."

"I will *not* let you melt me," she practically yelled at him.

"Is that a possibility?"

"Not any more. You lost your chance."

He shook his head. "I won't accept that answer."

"Too bad, because I—"

He took her by the arms and drew her in for a kiss.

She whimpered from the painful pleasure filling her chest. Her heart hammered, a staccato drumming of both optimism and desolation. She clutched the collar of his jacket, trying to ground herself.

It was pointless. The moment his lips touched hers she was lost.

He slowly brought the kiss in for a landing, nuzzling her cheek and neck before saying, "In the past, I've been with women who were princesses, women who sat back and expected me to save them. I put myself in the same situation with you, but the difference was I *wanted* to save you. Only you don't need saving, and I realize I'd rather have a partner, someone who'll hold her equal footing in the relationship."

"That's what I was offering you."

"I know that now."

"And you offered me a job." It still stung.

"You seemed to really like the database work you did. I wanted to give you something that'd make you happy."

"A baby would make me happy."

"Okay."

She glared at him. "That's not funny. Don't joke with me. It's cruel."

"I'm not joking."

She stared him in the eye. He gazed back solemnly, levelly, letting her see he was serious. Letting her see everything he was offering.

Hope began to overtake the regret. "A baby isn't all I want," she said carefully.

"I'll give you the moon."

Chanel barked, as if reinforcing the offer.

Kristin smiled at the dog before returning her at-

tention to the man. "I just want you."

He kissed her again. "That's what I've been trying to tell you. You already have me."

Chapter Twenty-five

THE DOORBELL BUZZED at dawn.

Sam glanced at the time. Fine—it wasn't dawn, but it was damn early, especially after a sleepless night.

He rolled out of bed, bleary-eyed with a hollow feeling in his chest. None of that was new, at least not since Lola had stopped seeing him.

He missed her. Bad.

She wasn't returning his calls. He'd even gone and tried to see her, but she'd been out and she hadn't answered the note he'd left her. She was all he thought about, every minute of every day.

He loved her.

It was so obvious now. But he'd screwed up, and she'd written him off. Which, frankly, annoyed the hell out of him. If she was going to storm off every time he did something stupid, they were going to have a rocky road ahead of them.

The buzzer sounded again, long and insistent.

"I'm coming," he yelled as he scrounged for a T-shirt.

"I got it, Daddy," Madison yelled back from down the hall.

He heard her racing down the stairs. A garbled conversation. The door slamming. The surprisingly loud stomping of her feet on the stairs. "You've got a package, Daddy."

He found her in the living room, hovering over a box, Dirty Dancing playing in the background. "You're watching that movie again?"

"I *love* it." She pointed at the package. "That's for you."

"Who is it from?" he asked, picking up the box. Heavy. He shook it, and something large shifted from one side to the other. On the label, there was only his name and address—no sender name or information.

Madison jumped up and down. "Just open it."

He picked a corner of the packing tape and ripped it all off. He opened the flaps and frowned at the contents.

"Let me see." She moved the box so she could peer inside. "That's from Lola!"

"One of her books." The book she'd been working on, he'd bet. It was a thick stack of paper bound by a rubber band. The cover sheet read:

Now and Forever:
Louise and Sawyer
-- By
Lola Carmichael

Was it done? He flipped through the first few pages. Why had she sent it to him?

As if reading his mind, Madison said, "Remember when I asked you if you could do something to get Lola back, and you said that you'd tried but she wasn't meeting you halfway?"

"Yeah."

"I think she's meeting you halfway."

"Maybe," he said, staring at the manuscript. "I need coffee."

"I'll make it, Daddy. You sit here and read." His daughter ran into the kitchen.

He could hear her pour beans and grind them. Madison's coffee was better than his own. Whenever he asked her how she made it so good, she just shrugged and said it must be because she made it with love.

He adored that kid.

Pushing the throw blanket she'd been using aside, he sat, propped his feet on the coffee table, and began to read.

He barely noticed when Madison set a mug on the table and sat down next to him to resume watching *Dirty Dancing*. His coffee went cold. His back got stiff from not moving. Madison drifted in and out of the living room without disturbing him. His stomach grumbled with hunger. But he read straight through, getting up once to go to the bathroom.

Louise and Sawyer were obviously he and Lola. Sam recognized the fictionalized versions of some of their conversations. He laughed at the banter, and he got hot at the sexy parts.

Mostly, he remembered how great it was with Lola. He *missed* her. *So bad.*

He read until he got to the last chapter, which was blank—except for a handwritten note:

I don't know how the story ends. Do Louise and Sawyer get together? I want them to, but I'm not sure how to write the scene. Maybe you have ideas...

Actually he had no ideas, but he'd figure some-

thing out—something worthy of a romance hero. He set the book aside and hurried to shower. He had a heroine to woo. ASAP, because their forever was on the line.

Sam and Madison stood in front of the mirror, staring at his outfit. "I look gay," he said finally.

"No you don't." She frowned.

He tugged at the tight, short-sleeved black shirt. It'd have looked okay if it hadn't been unbuttoned to his navel. Add the tight black pants and leather jacket and he looked like a gigolo. "Are you sure?"

"She totally loves *Dirty Dancing*, and you look just like Johnny." She squinted at him. "Or maybe Johnny's dad."

He scrubbed her head. "Gee. Thanks."

She giggled, ducking away from his reach. Then she sobered, worrying her lip. "This is going to work, isn't it?"

He lifted her chin. "You like Lola that much?"

"I love her," she said with a child's simplicity.

He nodded. He did too. "I'll win her back."

"Don't forget the music, Daddy." She handed

him her iPod and the portable speaker setup from her room.

"Right." He grinned. "This is going to be good. You ready to do this?"

"Let go get her back!" Madison high-fived him as she marched out ahead of him.

On the way to Lola's, Madison pantomimed Lola's part as Sam went over the plan again. They cheered each other, high-fived some more, and generally whooped it up.

Until they arrived.

A worried silence settled in the car as they stared up at her apartment building. The sign on the ground-level store seemed to mock him: *Outta My Gourd*.

Damn straight, he was. He tugged at the shirt again.

"Put on your sunglasses, Daddy." Madison opened the door and got out.

"Right," he muttered, slipping them on. It was foggy in Laurel Heights, and with the sunglasses it was like night.

At Madison's urging, he set up the iPod and speaker on the trunk of the car. He tested it to make

sure it worked and then gave Madison a thumbs-up.

Lifting her little chin and squaring her thin shoulders, she marched to the building's intercom. He smiled at the way she took her part in this so seriously. He remembered the way she said she loved Lola, and his heart did a funny flop.

Madison pressed the button. There was a pause and then the hiss of Lola answering. "Yes?"

His daughter inched close to the speaker and yelled. "Lola!"

"Madison? Is that you?"

"Yes. I'm downstairs."

"I kind of guessed that since you're calling me on my intercom."

Sam grinned at Lola's subtle sarcasm.

"What I don't understand," she continued, "is why you're here."

"I need you," his daughter said, just like they'd practiced.

"I'll be right down," Lola answered without hesitation.

Madison turned around and pumped two fists in the air. She ran over to him. "*Go,* Daddy."

When Lola rushed out of the building a moment

later, he was standing on the sidewalk, hand outstretched, waiting for her.

She stumbled to a stop. "Sam? If you're here, then why—"

Madison hit play, and "Time of My Life" poured onto Sacramento Street.

Lola blinked at Madison, and then turned her beautiful blue eyes onto him.

Sam stepped forward, his hand still out. "I have an idea about how your story ends."

"Do you?"

He heard the hope and longing and love in her voice, and a knot inside his chest unraveled. He nodded, walking toward her, waiting for her to accept his invitation. "It's brilliant, even if it's slightly plagiarized."

A smile flirted with her lips. "Are you trying to get me into trouble?"

"Definitely."

She looked at his hand, took a deep breath, stepped forward, and put her palm in his.

He twirled her around into his arms. Pressed chest to chest, he brushed her hair out of her eyes, reveling in the feel of her. *This* was right. "I shouldn't

have withheld Jennifer's deal from you. I'm sorry about that."

"And I'm sorry I didn't trust you," she said. "We share equal responsibility."

"Yes, we do, and I want it to be like that from now on."

"Where you piss me off, and I piss you off in return?"

He tugged her hair. "I'm trying to channel my most sincere Patrick Swayze, and you're being a wiseass."

"You make a great Patrick Swayze. Hot." She pulled the sunglasses off his face and tucked them into his shirt pocket. "That's better."

"You didn't answer me."

"Yes."

"Yes, you didn't answer me?"

She rolled her eyes. "Yes, I want 'from now on.' I love you."

"I love you, too." He kissed her softly, and then kissed her again more deeply because he could. Because he was happy. Because she was his.

The enthusiastic clapping invaded both their consciousnesses at the same time. They looked up to find a crowd of onlookers cheering them on. The loudest stood in the doorway of the gourd store, a bohemian looking woman in a bright skirt with a wickedly loud whistle.

Madison ran to them and threw her arms around them both. They squeezed her between them. He closed his eyes, simply grateful. Simply happy with his life for the first time ever.

Madison looked up at them, excitement written all over her face. "For the record, I'd like a little sister, but if it's a brother, I'm okay with that, too. And maybe you can give me one soon? I'm kinda getting old."

Lola grinned at Sam. He didn't know if she was okay with more kids—he didn't know if *he* was—but he could see she was definitely okay with the act of it. He winked at her.

His daughter gasped. "Daddy, you missed the best part of the plan."

He groaned. "Do I have to?"

"Yes." She ran back to the car and turned the music up. Then she crossed her arms and impatiently tapped her foot.

He turned to Lola. "I was supposed to sweep you away with my dancing."

Lola hugged him close. "You got moves in you, Patrick?"

"I've got all the moves you need." He pulled her close and began to dirty dance her along Sacramento Street's sidewalk. Their audience hooted and hollered as he led her in a random series steps.

Throwing her head back, she laughed. "This is the best ending ever."

"Sweetheart"—he pulled her even closer and whispered in her ear, just for her—"this is only the beginning."

Epilogue

LOLA TOOK THE glass of champagne Sam handed her and thanked him by saying, "I'm not wearing underwear."

His own glass, which had been on its way to his mouth, stopped abruptly, and his gaze fell to her strapless dress. "None?"

"Not one scrap of lace." Sipping her drink, she looked around the Presidio's Log Cabin, which Eve had transformed into a wedding wonderland, with white flowers and candles. Toward the back there was a small altar set up with chairs circling around it. Eve had told her she and Treat wanted to be surrounded by their family and friends as they exchanged their vows. "It's beautiful in here, isn't it?"

"Yes." He leaned toward her, brushing her hair from her shoulder. "But I'd rather discuss your underwear."

She shivered, feeling the tug of his desire. "There's nothing to discuss. Literally."

"I'd like to see that for myself." He hand ran down her back and over the curve of her butt.

"Hey there." Gwen bounded up to them, dragging her boyfriend Rick along. She winked at Lola. "Is this your new stud muffin?"

"Stud muffin?" Sam asked.

"Just go with it." Lola patted his chest. "Gwen has a way with words. And pumpkins."

Her friend snorted.

"This is Gwen and Rick," she said. "And this is—"

"Sam Taylor," Rick finished for her.

Sam blinked in surprise. "Have we met?"

"I had Rick run a report on you," Gwen said without shame.

Lola groaned. "*Gwen.*"

"What? I was concerned about you." Her friend turned to Sam. "Rick is a private detective, and he knows everything about you, so you better behave."

"What if I don't want him to behave?" Lola protested.

Rick chuckled and offered his hand to Sam. "They're nutty, but they're ours."

"Amen to that." The men shook hands and promptly sidled away to discuss football.

Lola accepted a mini quiche from a passing waiter. "Eve outdid herself."

"She lives for stuff like this. Personally, I'd have eloped to Vegas and had Elvis marry me."

"There's something lovely about being married in front of your family and friends though."

"Says the romance writer." Gwen grinned and poked her. "I can just see the insanity when you decide to take the plunge."

Actually, she and Sam had been talking about going someplace far away and tropical and getting married in a private ceremony—just them and Madison. Lola realized it was all she wanted—that and the perfect dress. A girl shouldn't compromise too much.

She just wished her mom could go, too, but her mother wouldn't be able to attend even if they stayed local. Her health hadn't bounced back. The doctors were perplexed by how she'd steadily deteriorated over the past weeks. She'd become a shell of her former self, even more withdrawn and silent.

She never knitted anymore.

Lola had taken Sam to meet her that morning for

the first time. She'd had to keep her crying to a minimum as Sam had assured her mom he'd love Lola forever and always take care of her. As he'd made the promise, her mom's hand had twitched, and Lola knew Sally had heard his vow.

But she shook those thoughts off. Now was the time for happiness.

"Did you see the cake?" Gwen asked, pointing to the spot where the confection was set up. "It's four layers of *amazing*. Daniela Rossi is pastry chef to the stars for a reason."

"I was really looking forward to seeing her shop, but it isn't open yet. It's strange. Has she mentioned to you what the hold up is?"

Gwen shook her head. "She doesn't talk to me much. She mostly hangs out with Eve. She's a little standoffish, but my theory is that she's shy."

"I think she's lonely," Lola said, spotting the woman, who suddenly appeared with last minute garnishes for the cake. "She seems sad and wary."

"You know who's not sad or lonely?" Gwen pointed to the opposite end of the room. "Kristin."

They both grinned as they watched Kristin trap her new beau in a dark corner. He looked like he

didn't mind—like he was precisely where he wanted to be. Who could blame him? Kristin was smart and funny, and tonight she looked beyond sexy in her little black dress.

Olivia walked over and slipped her arm through Gwen's. "I've been sent to inform the best man needs to report for duty, and that the rest of us need to sit down."

Rick's head perked up. "That's me." He kissed Gwen and hurried to find his best friend, the groom, and the rest of them ambled up to the front to take their seats.

Lola stared at Olivia's belly as they sat down. She tried to picture herself round with a baby inside. Madison was quite vocal about her desire for a little brother or sister. Lola pictured a little boy with Sam's grin and thought maybe.

Maybe.

The Vivaldi violin concerto began, and everyone held their breath, waiting.

Eve's maid of honor, Freya, strode down the aisle, her long-legged gait sure and her smile delighted. She winked at Treat and Rick before taking her place next to where the bride would be standing. Lola had met the tall redhead the week before at the bachelorette party and had liked her instantly. She looked forward to getting to know her better.

Then Eve entered in a long silky sheath.

Instead of watching her friend, Lola turned around and watched Treat's expression as he saw his bride for the first time. He looked in awe.

He looked in love.

Lola sighed. It was lovely.

Sam smiled at her, caressing her palm with his thumb. In his eyes there was promise—a promise for later, at home.

A promise for the future.

Don't miss the rest of the Laurel Heights series!

Perfect For You #1
Close To You #2
Return To You #3
Looking For You #4
Dream Of You #5

Also fall in love with Kate Perry's sexful, playful novels of family and love including *Playing Doctor* and *Playing for Keeps*...

Playing Doctor

After catching her research partner-slash-fiancé with the intern, Dr. Daphne Donovan returns home to lick her wounds and figure out how to fix her life. It doesn't take a genius to figure it out: being an uber-brilliant Doogie Howser has made her life miserable while all the normal people she knows are happy and content.

There's only one thing to do: become normal. No more being the wunderkind of childhood disease research. All she wants is a regular nine to five job, two-point-five children, a white picket fence, and a blue collar husband.

Except normal isn't all it's cracked up to be, especially after she meets Ulysses Gray. Gray is everything she doesn't want: smart, incredibly handsome, and a doctor--just like her ex-fiancé. She wants to deny him--and herself--but she can't resist playing doctor...

Playing for Keeps

Since her mother's death more than fifteen years before, Grace Connors has been the matriarch of her family. She's put her own dreams on hold to raise her younger sisters and keep her ex-marine father in line.

So when her sister Nell decides to get married, it's on Grace to make it a wedding their mother would have been proud of. It can't be hard to organize a party, right?

But then everything falls apart, including her budding romance with her sexy best friend Pete.

Caught in the crossfire with the enemy at her back, will Grace be able to fix it all before she becomes a casualty of love?

Legend of Kate

Kate has tangoed at midnight with a man in blue furry chaps, dueled with flaming swords in the desert, and strutted on bar tops across the world and back. She's been kissed under the Eiffel Tower, had her butt pinched in Florence, and been serenaded in New Orleans. But she found Happy Ever After in San Francisco with her Magic Man.

Kate's the bestselling author of the Laurel Heights Novels, as well as the Family and Love and Guardians of Destiny series. She's been translated into several languages and is quite proud to say she's big in Slovenia. All her books are about strong, independent women who just want love.

Most days, you can find Kate in her favorite café, working on her latest novel. Sometimes she's wearing a tutu. She may or may not have a jeweled dagger strapped to her thigh...

Made in the USA
Lexington, KY
09 January 2014